A Precious COMMODITY

A *Precious* COMMODITY

Sylvia M. Stachura

Copyright © 2024 by Sylvia M. Stachura.

All rights reserved. No part of this publication may be reproduced, distributed, or transmitted in any form or by any means, including photocopying, recording, or other electronic or mechanical methods, without the prior written permission of the author, except in the case of brief quotations embodied in critical reviews and certain other noncommercial uses permitted by copyright law.

This is a work of fiction. Names, characters, places and incidents either are products of the author's imagination or are used fictitiously. Any resemblance to actual events or locales or persons, living or dead, is entirely coincidental.

Printed in the United States of America

ISBN 979-8-89114-092-9 (hc)
ISBN 979-8-89114-091-2 (sc)
ISBN 979-8-89114-093-6 (e)

Library of Congress Control Number: 2024912792

2024.10.08

MainSpring Books
5901 W. Century Blvd
Suite 750
Los Angeles, CA, US, 90045

www.mainspringbooks.com

Acknowledgements

I would like to express my appreciation and special thanks to Christopher Hernandez, the Marketing Executive of Main Spring Books, for his professional guidance and dedication for his effort in turning my book into a hardcover novel. I would also like to express my gratitude to John Green, the Project Coordinator, as well as Marshall Evans, for their effort and valuable support.

Dedication

This book is dedicated to my beloved husband, Ed and my precious children, Jeffrey my son and Joelle my daughter, all of whom have encouraged me in this endeavor of my book. I love them dearly.

Prologue

MacGregor Stone was a man who dedicated his life to the pharmaceutical business; through which he had become a powerful magnate. It was difficult to think that someone of his magnitude was now so dangerously near death.

It had happened so quickly. He had always been so vital and filled with energy, inspiring others with his spirited leadership. Now he was suddenly helpless in a semicomatose state, his life hanging in the delicate balance. What if he did not pull through? What would life be like without him?

These thoughts reached troubling proportions as his wife, Lenore, sat rigidly with her hands clenched in her lap. Her face was pale and showed lines of stress that had become etched more vividly, revealing her deep anxiety. She sighed with weariness and frustration, closing her eyes, trying to block out the grim reality that was confronting her.

They had been married for forty-five wonderful and fulfilling years, far longer than most couples, but even so, she could not imagine life going on without him. This could not happen, not yet. It would be an anachronism, a mistiming of events. She needed more time. But how much of it would be allowed them? How could she ever find peace without him, not even knowing the full impact of the events that were to follow? The family would be threatened and would find out that the worst betrayal had come from within.

Chapter 1

Mac, live, please live. I need you now more than ever. You're much too vital, my love, to give up so easily, Lenore Stone prayed silently as she sat in the racing ambulance.

Above the pandemonium of midday traffic, the persistent electronic whine of the ambulance siren was heard as it sped toward the hospital. The movement of traffic became disturbed and was brought to a halt by the encroaching vehicle. Its spinning red lights elicited an awesome warning that an emergency was taking place.

Inside the ambulance, MacGregor Stone fought for his every breath to sustain life. The attendant checked his vital signs and gave the patient oxygen to ease his labored breathing.

The patient's wife, Lenore, began to chat nervously with the driver and was filled with much apprehension for her beloved husband, who appeared to be imminently approaching death.

"I kept encouraging him to see a doctor, but he kept putting it off." Lenore held a handkerchief in her hand and anxiously twisted it as she spoke. "Mac has had this cold for the past two weeks, and it seemed much worse this morning. He has also been having a lot of vague aches and pains for some time now, but after all, he is not a young man."

"Yes, ma'am," the driver acknowledged.

Mac Stone was brought in on a stretcher and was immediately taken to one of the examining rooms. Lenore was seated next to a receptionist, who obtained all the pertinent information.

At her first opportunity, Lenore made a quick call to her son, MacGregor Stone II, at Stone Pharmaceutical Laboratories, one of the largest of its kind in the nation. Her son, whom she referred to as Greg, was president of the company, and her husband held the position of chairman of the board.

"I'm sorry," the receptionist replied, "but Mr. Stone is away at a luncheon meeting and isn't expected back for some time."

Feeling a bit agitated, Lenore left a message for her son, telling him that his father was in the hospital.

In a lovely two-story contemporary home situated in a wooded suburb of Boston, Melanie Lambert had made several attempts to reach her mother by phone, finally leaving her a message. She was planning an art gallery benefit and needed to check on several names and addresses with Lenore. Melanie did a lot of volunteer work at the art gallery and was placed in charge of organizing fundraising events. Finally, she decided to relinquish her efforts to reach her mother and resolutely waited for her to return her call. As she did so, the phone suddenly rang, giving her a start.

"Melanie, I have some distressing news." Lenore sounded extremely agitated as she spoke to her daughter. "Your father became very ill today and had to be taken by ambulance to the hospital."

"What happened, Mom? Do you know what's wrong with Dad?"

"Well, he woke up rather late this morning and was terribly disoriented. He didn't seem to know where he was and began to act strangely. In fact, he could hardly speak, and what he did say was very incoherent. I'm afraid that he may have had a stroke. And that awful cold he's had for the past couple of weeks . . ."

"Calm down, Mother. We can't have you getting ill too. I'm sure Dad will be just fine. Has Dr. Brooks been notified?"

"Yes, Melanie, Dr. Brooks was with him. They've taken him for some tests. It'll be a while before the results are known." Lenore paused for a moment, gathering her thoughts. "I haven't been able to get in touch with your brother."

"Don't worry. I'll try to reach him just before I leave for the hospital. Relax, Mom, I'll see you in a little while."

Melanie hung up the phone and sat motionless, thinking back to the conversation she just had. Her father had always been so healthy. She couldn't imagine him being so ill. His name, Stone, had always seemed to signify his very state of being. He was the foundation on which the family rested, always dependable, full of strength, wisdom, and courage. She found it difficult to think of him as ever being vulnerable in any way, with only one exception: he had much emotional capital invested in his family. His love was very strong. Under certain circumstances, Melanie thought, it could be extremely unbearable for him and possibly even dangerous if they were threatened.

As a little girl, she had been the light of his life. Mac would have loved to devote more time to her, but the pharmaceutical business kept him away a great deal. To make up for this personal deficiency, he spoiled his little daughter by showering her with gifts and favors at every opportunity. No request was ever too extraordinary in Mac's estimation. So when Melanie had married Alan Lambert, a bright and young, but struggling, lawyer, she had asked her father to help expedite his career. In response, Mac began to give Alan small legal problems to manage for the company. After Alan had sufficiently proven himself, Mac hired him as his chief legal counsel, giving Alan's career a tremendous thrust upward.

In Melanie's brother, Greg, however, Mac saw a reflection of himself. It was comparable to gazing in a mirror and observing time suddenly stripped away by thirty years. He demanded the same perfection in Greg as he did of himself. His son was an extension of his own being, the one who would continue the fulfillment of his dreams and expectations and, finally, to assume the office of president of Stone Pharmaceutical Laboratories, the position that Greg now held successfully.

Mac had great pride in his son and generously expressed it to everyone but Greg. He erroneously believed that his son might become a victim of overconfidence, taking undue risks with the company. As a result, the business would suffer.

However, Greg instinctively knew his father's true feelings. Besides, his mother gave him enough praise to make up for any shortcomings. Nevertheless, Mac had instilled in his son the belief that his passion for the company was his constant and foremost duty.

Chapter 2

At a seafood restaurant in the famous Faneuil Hall Marketplace, Greg Stone was having lunch with Renée Bordeaux, one of his top salespeople. Renée had won a sales award last year and was discussing another large account, which she was confident that she was going to land soon.

Greg was more than proud of her and admired her in numerous ways. She was intelligent, warm, and gregarious with the strikingly beautiful, dark features of the French.

Renée had left France three years ago after a marriage that had failed and came to Boston for a new beginning. She was hired by Stone Pharmaceutical Labs and devoted all her energies to her work in an effort to forget her tumultuous marriage. She wanted and needed to overcome the pain she had suffered with the separation and, finally, the ensuing divorce.

Renée began her career at Stone Labs as an assistant sales manager but, within a relatively short time, demonstrated her capabilities with the major clients. She took it upon herself to land a good-sized account and, as a result, the assistant was removed from her title. After having won the sales award, she was then brought to the fine scrutiny of the president of the company, MacGregor Stone II. From a distance, she admired his rugged handsomeness that was suggestive of good health and strength. He had a well-proportioned and imposing appearance, blond wavy hair that was becoming tinged with gray, intense blue eyes, and a generous smile. Renée knew that he was married and wondered what it was like to be loved by such a powerful man. Was he as demanding a lover as he was an administrator? The first time that he had spoken to her, after one of the weekly sales conferences, she felt rather light-headed, unable to believe that she had finally acquired his full attention. That was three days ago. This morning, he had called her into his office and had asked her to meet with him over lunch.

She sat across from him in the restaurant, observing his mannerisms as he ate. How typically American, she thought, juggling his fork back and forth from right hand to left each time he cut into a piece of filet of sole. What a wasted effort! One would think that, by now, the Americans would have conformed to the European method of eating with the left hand while cutting with the right. But why was she being so critical? Through her eyes, he had always been a paragon of accomplishment and perfection. Was it a defense mechanism to mask her true feelings? Or was she so overwhelmed by his very presence that, in order to make him more accessible, she found it necessary to erase some of his magnitude by taking him down from his pedestal?

Greg looked at Renée, suddenly noticing her stare.

"Is anything wrong? Do I have a piece of lemon peel stuck to the tip of my nose?" he teased and continued to look at her, smiling broadly.

"No," she replied, turning her eyes downward to escape his and feeling the warmth rushing to her cheeks. She did not wish to have him know that she had been scrutinizing him from across the table. Looking up again and returning his smile, she was able to regain her composure and said, "A lemon peel could only enhance rather than detract. It would bring out the color of your hair, Monsieur Stone."

Greg gave her a long and approving look. His blue eyes were warm and caressing, and he appeared to be somewhat animated. No woman had ever attracted him this way or distracted him so much since his wife, Vanessa, when they first met more than twenty years ago. The idea of being unfaithful had never occurred to him until that moment—but only for that moment. After it had passed, he spoke.

"I think that it's time to discuss that Reynolds account. I'd like to clear up a few details with you so that we're both on the right track—or at least on the same one."

"Yes, I suppose we should discuss business. That is why you asked me to lunch, is it not, Monsieur Stone?"

Greg ignored her question and immediately dove into the financial aspect of the new account that the company was hoping to acquire.

After much lengthy discussion, Renée pointed out that she felt the Reynolds people might be holding back in anticipation of a better offer. But she let him know that she was definitely on top of the situation.

"I will do everything I can to win them over," Renée assured.

"I have every confidence in your ability, Renée. You won't fail me. You haven't in the past, and you won't this time either."

His vitality was contagious, and she believed what he said.

"With you behind me, how can I lose?" She gave him a quick wink and reached for her napkin as a sign that she was finished with lunch.

"It's getting late," Greg said, quickly getting his wallet out to pay for the check. "On the way out, I'd like to call the office to see if there were any important messages."

Greg paid the check and then left to make the call. By the time he reached for his cell phone, Greg found that he was filled with an abundance of nervous energy. In fact, he walked out of the dining area of the restaurant very briskly, leaving Renée a few paces behind. He couldn't remember when he last felt so disconcerted.

When he checked his messages on his cell phone and also checked with his secretary, she related several messages to him, including the one regarding his father being hospitalized. He instructed his secretary to postpone all appointments that were scheduled for the remainder of the day. Greg felt it was imperative that he leave for the hospital immediately.

After returning to where Renée waited for him, Greg reiterated to her the message regarding his father's illness.

"I'll drop you off at the office and head on to the hospital."

Looking fully into his eyes, she was filled with compassion. "I'm so sorry to hear this, Monsieur Stone. I sincerely hope that there is nothing seriously wrong with your father."

"My father has enjoyed good health for most of his life. Since he's in the hospital, I'm afraid that it is serious. He was never one to coddle himself. In fact, he dislikes hospitals intensely."

Greg dropped Renée off at the main door of Stone Labs and sped in the direction of the hospital. As he arrived, Greg walked through the doors and spotted his sister Melanie waiting for him in the main lobby.

She greeted him, and they proceeded up to the Intensive Care Unit where Mac had been admitted.

"Greg, Dad had a CAT scan earlier which showed that he had a mild stroke. Dr. Brooks gave Mom the dreadful details. Mom and I haven't been able to get through to Dad. He's just not himself. Dr. Brooks also said that his chest X-ray showed some pneumonia in the left lung. I'm really frightened, but I don't want Mom to know. It'll only upset her more. And she's in a bit of a state now."

They walked into the waiting room, where they found Lenore Stone speaking with Dr. Brooks. "Is there anything that can be done for him? I feel so helpless not being able to communicate with Mac."

Dr. Brooks gently took her arm and seated Lenore in one of the stuffed chairs. "Everything is being done, Mrs. Stone. He's being fed intravenously and is receiving medication. I'll order more tests for tomorrow morning. He seems to be resting comfortably, and his breathing isn't as labored now that he's receiving oxygen. I suggest that you relax for a while."

Dr. Brooks looked up just as Greg and Melanie approached. "Greg, it's been a long time since I've seen you," Dr. Brooks said as he rose and extended a handshake to Greg.

Greg smiled and responded in kind. "Yes, Richard, I guess it's been a couple of years. The lab has been keeping me busy. It's good to see you again, but I wish that we were meeting under more pleasant circumstances."

"So do I, Greg. But for now, I want you and your sister, Melanie, to take care of your mother for me. Make sure that she gets some rest." He then walked out of the waiting room and over to the nurses' station, giving instructions to one of the nurses. After checking on Mac, he went into one of the elevators.

Melanie sat down next to her mother and tried to comfort her. She then motioned to Greg to go into Mac's room.

Upon entering the room, Greg was filled with apprehension. He wondered what he would find and, whatever it was, if he would be able to face it.

His father lay there with his eyes closed and appeared to be asleep. There were several different instruments to which he was attached, monitoring his heart rate and blood pressure, and an IV containing a saline solution along with an anticoagulant and antibiotic being fed into his arm. He was also receiving oxygen through a nasal cannula. This shell of a man, totally vulnerable and at the mercy of these monitors and tubes that were inadvertently helping to sustain his life, to Greg, had merely a vague resemblance to the strong and vigorous father he knew. He now appeared very old and frail, and his skin tone blended with the gray in his hair. There were hollows in his cheeks much deeper than he had remembered.

Greg slowly approached the bed. He reached over and cupped Mac's hand with his. "Dad, it's Greg. Are you awake?" For a moment, there was no response. Greg felt compelled to arouse him, needing to see signs of life. His emotions reverted to almost that of a child. "Dad, look at me. It's your son, Greg. Say something so that I know you recognize me."

Mac opened his eyes and saw his son standing over him. He tried to speak but was unable to form the words properly. He made another attempt but again the words came out inaudibly. Then his eyes closed, and he slipped back into a semicomatose state.

Greg stood silently by the bed for a moment in deep contemplation. He then turned and walked slowly out of the room.

In the waiting room, Lenore and Melanie sat quietly, each engrossed in their own thoughts, as Greg returned, looking somewhat anguished.

"He's lost his ability to speak. I wasn't able to get anything out of him. I'm not even sure that he recognized me," Greg exclaimed.

"I know," Melanie replied. "Dad has been that way apparently all day. Mom and I tried to get him to speak but have had no luck. Mom says that he woke up this morning not knowing where he was."

"Yes, that's right," Lenore interrupted. "Your father simply hasn't been himself today. Dr. Brooks said that it would take a few days before we know the actual effects he has suffered as a result of the stroke. He said that the pneumonia is of primary concern right now. Hopefully, it won't progress any further."

Suddenly realizing how much time had elapsed, Lenore glanced at her watch and then at her two grown children. "I really appreciate and feel very comforted that you're both here with me at this time of crisis, but you do have families of your own who need your attention as well."

Greg was the first to speak. "Vanessa was going to be in a golf tournament at the country club today, and I don't know if she's returned home as yet. And your granddaughter, Marissa, went along to watch. She was scheduled for a tennis lesson this afternoon. I'll try to have Van paged in the event that she's back in the club house. Then, Mom, I'll have to leave."

"That'll be fine, Greg. Give them my love." She then leaned her cheek into his. "See you later, dear." Turning toward her daughter, she said, "And what about you, Melanie? Were you able to reach Alan at the law firm?"

"Yes, Mom, I spoke to him before coming over to the hospital. He said that he would be home early and would make sure that the boys had their dinner and were not in combat with one another. So I'm free to stay with you awhile."

"Mark and Derek are not that argumentative, Melanie. I think they get along quite well from what I've observed. At fifteen, life can be very difficult, especially if one has to share everything with one's identical twin brother. You're simply too close to the situation to be a good judge. You've got to be more objective and try to see their side occasionally, Melanie."

"I know, Mom, but that's very difficult to accomplish when you're thrown in the middle of a battlefield. It's almost impossible to come out of it unscathed!"

"Melanie, you certainly do exaggerate. Those boys are a source of tremendous pride and joy to your father and me—they always have been, and I'm sure that they always will be. They've done well in school and have never been in any kind of trouble."

"You're right, Mom. They must simply be reacting to me, always competing for my attention, which is not always of a positive nature." Melanie then rose from her chair. "Enough of this analysis. Let's go down to the coffee shop and see what's cooking. I'm suddenly starved!"

In the hospital lobby, Greg tried to reach his wife with his cell phone. Since she was not answering, he called the desk and had her paged. The voice on the loud speaker reverberated, "Vanessa Wilder Stone, Vanessa Wilder Stone, please come to the front desk."

Greg was not receiving any acknowledgement. He then decided to leave for home. The traffic at five o'clock was typically bumper-to-bumper in an unending procession, traveling at a very tedious pace.

Inside one of the cars, immersed in the procession, Greg could not get his thoughts away from his father, the invincible MacGregor Stone. That's what he was known as throughout the company, his company whose arms reached out to all parts of the country and Canada as well. And if Greg had his way, they would reach out to various parts of the world.

Greg was very enterprising and wanted more than his father had ever dreamed. He had been nurtured by his father from early youth to become the magnate he was today. Mac saw to it that his son's priorities were in the proper perspective. Greg's studies were always of primary importance. After all his assignments were completed, he was then, and only then, allowed to participate in any extracurricular activity of his choice. There were times when he felt frustrated by this, especially during his teens, when he would have preferred a more unrestricted social life. Greg looked forward to weekends, the only time he was given free rein. But even on occasional Saturday mornings, he would accompany his father to the lab and sometimes meet with a client for lunch. This gave Greg the opportunity to observe his father's technique in winning over the prospective client's account. His summers were also spent learning the pharmaceutical business. In this way, Greg became well primed for his eventual and ultimate position at Stone Laboratories that he now held—president of the company.

Greg felt that he had worked hard and devoted a great deal of time and energy to deserve this prestigious position. He could never be accused by his subordinates or by anyone else that he was given this position merely because he was the boss's son. It had not been an easy climb. It required tremendous dedication, sacrifice, and enormous self-discipline to reach such a high entrepreneurial accomplishment.

MacGregor Stone II was, beyond a shadow of a doubt, his father's son. They both shared a distinctive need for power, for being in control, and both had an inherent ability to acquire great wealth. The only difference was that the senior Stone was the more conservative of the two. The younger Stone wanted to broaden the company's base. Presently, it held leadership in three major areas, but Greg felt that its product base was still too narrow. He had suggested on several occasions the need for new areas in which the company could expand, each requiring the development of new drugs. He also wanted to tap the European market, a strong possibility, but his father had objected, along with several other members of the board of directors.

Mac had become more conservative than ever in the past couple of years. Greg felt that he was slowing down, and rightfully so, due to his age. He considered the possibility that his father might retire soon, even though there was never any mention of retirement. He had also mellowed a great deal, becoming far more approachable than he had been in his younger days. However, Greg had never anticipated this illness, which had become so incapacitating. But then, no man is indestructible and neither was his father.

Greg was now becoming filled with guilt. Was he subconsciously wishing his father out of the way so that he could proceed with his new strategy? He had great love for his father; he would never wish him any ill will. However, Greg was able to admit to himself that he had a grand ambition for the growth of the company. He realized that he wanted it with all his being. To attain this end, could he be so unscrupulous as to go behind his father's back and propel his plan through now that his father was not able to vote on the decision?

Finally, out of the maddening traffic, Greg turned onto the private road that led to his magnificent home. It was beautiful and picturesque, overlooking a breathtaking countryside that nature had painted in various shades of green, yellow, and red. The flower beds were impeccably manicured with a riot of color in every direction, framing the house, and seemed to glimmer in the late sunshine.

The yardman seems to have surpassed himself with the gardening this year, Greg thought as he pulled his Mercedes into the garage. *He's finally earning the exorbitant wages that he's being paid*. As he walked into the house, Greg encountered his nineteen-year-old daughter, Marissa, who greeted him with a kiss.

Marissa was tall and slender, with her mother's dark wavy hair that came past her shoulders. She had her father's enormous eyes that were a deep violet blue. In the fall, she would be going into her sophomore year at Boston College.

"Hi, Dad!" Marissa exclaimed. "Guess what, Mom came in a mere second in the ladies golf tournament today. Isn't that an awful letdown? Mrs. Winthrop, of all people, came in first! She can't even tell a wood from an iron."

"Well, honey, she apparently could today. Where's your mother?"

"Here I am, Greg," Vanessa replied as she came into the kitchen. "I was on the phone just a moment ago and heard from one of my friends at the club that someone had been paging me there late this afternoon. I had my cell phone turned off. Could it have been you?"

"Yes, I've been trying to reach you. I have some very unpleasant news. My dad had a stroke this morning and was taken to the hospital." Greg reiterated all that had transpired today at the hospital to the stunned faces of his wife and daughter. "You can both visit him tomorrow if you like. I'll meet you there later. But first, I think it's important that I meet with the board of directors to let them in on what has happened. We'll have to elect another chairman to take over in Dad's absence."

"Of course, we'll be there. This must be a terrible strain on your mother. She needs us all now to help her through this."

"I knew you'd be understanding, Vanessa. That's why Mom and Dad have always been so terribly fond of you. And having a favorite granddaughter present will be a perfect distraction, right, Marissa?" Greg mused as he glanced at his daughter with pride.

"I hate the thought of seeing Grandpa so ill. Poor Grandmother must be terribly upset. I'll go along with Mom," Marissa said resolutely, as she flopped herself into a chair.

By this time, Greg felt the need to stop dwelling on the subject of his father's illness. It had thrown him into a depressed state for several hours, and he now desperately needed to escape from his own thoughts. Decidedly, he moved the conversation to a topic that was more ethereal in nature. "So I hear that you came in second in the tournament today." Greg directed the question to his wife.

"Yes, what a disappointment that was! I think that I sliced the ball once too often. And did you hear that Rhoda Winthrop took first place? She was one golfer whom I felt was not a threat to me in the least. She's been playing badly all summer."

"That's what is known in most circles as overconfidence," Greg replied with a teasing smile. "Never underestimate your competition for you may be fooled. The same holds true in business: never trust anyone completely. But, of course, in this case, Mrs. Winthrop was on a lucky streak."

"Mom wasn't playing her usual good game today either," suggested Marissa. "Maybe she sensed that something was wrong."

"You know what, Marissa, you may have a point," Vanessa acknowledged. "I didn't feel the nervous excitement that I generally feel in this situation. It must have been my intuition. When you've lived with a person for more than twenty years, you are able to sense things and many times are able to read the other's very thoughts and sometimes even finish his sentences."

"Gee, I don't know about that. Sounds rather spooky to me," Marissa replied. "I hope you're not able to read my thoughts. I like keeping a few secrets to myself."

The three of them bantered back and forth in a jovial conversation all through dinner that evening. It proved to be a tremendous anodyne for the tension and temporarily erased the earlier sadness.

Chapter 3

The morning was bleak and rainy. It had the kind of steady rain that would last for most of the day. The cloud-laden sky darkened the hope for a promising day ahead.

Greg walked into the board room and greeted all the members. Most of them knew that Mac was ill. News of such paramount significance generally circulated very quickly. Nevertheless, due to Mac's position as chairman of the board, Greg felt that an official announcement had to be made. An election had to take place for a temporary chairman to preside.

A nomination was made for David Warner, an intelligent, grayhaired man in his early fifties. Greg felt that he was a progressive type, loyal to the company, usually open to new ideas, and showed good business strategy. He was a good choice. Two other nominations were made, and then the election was held.

As Greg had expected, David Warner was the victor. After the meeting, all the members congratulated him and finally dispersed.

Greg went to his office to make several phone calls and took care of some important details that had been left undone yesterday. As he completed the signing of a few letters, the intercom buzzer suddenly startled him.

"Mr. Stone, Renée Bordeaux would like to see you," his secretary announced.

"Thank you. Send her in immediately," Greg replied.

Renée walked into the spacious office, looking very petite in contrast to the surroundings. The room was decorated with very bold, masculine furnishings richly carved in a mahogany wood finish. She looked very attractive in her well-tailored suit. It was very flattering to her, Greg thought admiringly, as she proceeded toward him.

Renée spoke first. "Monsieur Stone, I'd like to again express my condolences, and I sincerely hope that your father will be feeling better very soon."

"Thank you, Renée. He's having tests done this morning. We should have more information about his condition very soon. Hopefully, it'll all be good."

"I have some good news for you this morning that should cheer you up. The Reynolds account that we discussed over lunch yesterday looks very promising. I am to meet with Mr. Reynolds's assistant tomorrow to work out a couple of details. As I told you before, I will do everything possible to win him over. He gave me every indication that his company was very interested in us. I feel very confident that we will get the account." Renée's dark eyes sparkled and seemed to dance with excitement as she spoke about her possible victory.

Greg was captivated by her enthusiasm. "I was right to have faith in you, Renée. You're an excellent saleswoman. I'm confident that you will go very far."

"To say, an excellent woman would be much more satisfying." Renée looked at him coquettishly and observed his reaction. He appeared to be rather disconcerted, and it pleased her.

Greg hesitated a moment then answered. "Yes, I'm sure you are and an extraordinary one, at that."

Renée smiled at him contentedly. "I never had the opportunity to thank you for the wonderful lunch yesterday. You rushed off so quickly. Perhaps I could return the favor another time."

"Perhaps," Greg said, his eyes revealing an illuminated glow.

"Now I must get back to work and let you get back to yours. Au revoir, Monsieur Stone."

"See you later, Renée." Greg went back to the papers that were on his desk and continued to work, occasionally being distracted. His thoughts kept drifting back to his conversation with Renée. He found himself fascinated by her. She was lovely and enticing. He was not at all surprised that Renée was such a success in sales. After all, she possessed every attribute that was required and was able to use each one of them to her full advantage. He could not help but wonder, however, to what length she would go to win a client. He knew that she was pursuing a successful and highly profitable career that would eventually jettison her to a higher position.

* * *

The Intensive Care Unit was bustling with medical personnel. The large carts containing lunch trays filled with food made grating noises as they traversed the halls, making stops at almost every doorway.

Lenore Stone had spent a rather restless night in bed without her husband and a very anxious morning as well. She had arrived shortly after noon, since her husband was going to be having tests for most of the morning. As she walked into Mac's room, Lenore found him sound asleep, obviously exhausted from the morning experience.

The rain kept falling, making the day dark and dismal. Lenore walked the halls and then stopped to gaze through one of the windows in the waiting room. Rain depressed her and was now casting a gray shadow over the lush green summer tapestry outside. She saw windshield wipers on passing cars dancing back and forth as a metronome keeps the tempo for a piano player. People were running in different directions, trying to escape the rain that was now coming down in torrents. Some very casually walked past, well prepared and sheltered by an umbrella. Those were the smart ones, Lenore thought, the ones who were prepared to weather the storm.

Back in the hall near the nurses' station, Vanessa and her daughter, Marissa, encountered Dr. Brooks walking from the opposite direction. As he approached, Dr. Brooks greeted Vanessa first. He then took one step back and, with an amazed expression written on his face, looked at Marissa and said teasingly, "Be still, my foolish heart. She has the outward appearance of a woman, but she's still merely a child!"

"I'm not a child," Marissa said, laughing aloud with some embarrassment.

"Marissa, what a beauty you've become."

Astonished to see someone from her childhood whom she had almost forgotten, Marissa suddenly realized that this man speaking to her was Dr. Brooks. "Hi, Dr. Brooks, you remembered me!"

"Of course I remembered you, Marissa, but certainly not this way. It must be five years since I last saw you in my office. You've changed a lot since then! You must be approximately nineteen years old. Am I right?"

"You have a good memory, Dr. Brooks. Yes, I am nineteen."

At fourteen, Marissa requested that her mother find for her a female doctor. Being rather shy at the time, a male doctor was a source of embarrassment for her. Modesty had prevailed. Her mother had inquired among her friends and was given the name of a woman in her midthirties who Marissa was sure to like. She was Dr. Nancy Evans, a very warm and friendly person, who Marissa had grown very fond of and even considered her a friend. Vanessa was pleased that her daughter was able to discuss everything with the doctor. She realized that at a certain age, usually in her teens, a girl ceases confiding in her mother as she did as a little girl. Usually, all her secrets were shared with her peers. In Marissa's case, her best confidant was Dr. Evans. Her mother had chosen well.

Richard Brooks and Greg had grown up together and attended the same schools up until college. They had remained friends throughout the years, and Richard eventually became the younger Stone's family physician. Because he had proven himself to be an excellent doctor, the senior Stones also began to utilize his medical services.

Dr. Brooks was now attempting to track down Lenore in order to convey to her the results of the tests that were performed on Mac this morning. "Vanessa, have you seen Lenore today? I must speak to her."

"I haven't seen her as yet, but I'm sure that she's here."

As Lenore sat pensively in the waiting room, her daughter, Melanie, reached the hospital and discovered her there alone. Intuitively sensing her mother's sullen mood, Melanie began her conversation on a pleasant note. "Hi, Mom! How are you today? That outfit looks terrific on you. Is it new?"

"Oh, thank you, dear. No, it isn't new. I've had it for a few months. My intention was to look good for your father, but I really don't think that he'll notice."

"I know what you mean," Melanie replied. "As I reached the ICU, I peeked in on Dad, and he was snoring away. He almost sounded like a vacuum cleaner."

Lenore broke into laughter, and with it, she felt a release of tension. "You're good to have around, Melanie. I know that it's been a long time since I've said it, but I love you—more than ever."

"I know, Mom. I've never doubted it." Melanie paused for a moment to gather her thoughts and then continued. "Up until yesterday, when you called, my life has been on the upswing, as they say. Working at the art gallery, organizing and scheduling exhibits and fund-raising benefits, and having first choice at buying valuable artwork has all been very exciting and rewarding. Best of all, Alan's becoming senior partner in the law firm that's now known as Trent, Randolph, and Lambert was a wonderful and auspicious occasion. We'll always be grateful to Dad for his tremendous influence in Alan's career by making him legal counsel for Stone Labs. Because of all of this, we wanted to celebrate in some way. We've been so happy that we wanted to spread the joy around a bit. But today, I don't feel like celebrating anymore."

"Yes, I know what you mean," Lenore replied. "Your father's illness has changed my outlook on a lot of things. Just wondering what Dr. Brooks will have to say to us today."

"Then you haven't seen Dr. Brooks as yet."

Just at that moment, Dr. Brooks came walking into the waiting room followed by Vanessa and Marissa.

"Well, speak of the devil and he suddenly appears!" Melanie exclaimed as she turned toward the entrance to see Dr. Richard Brooks walking in.

He gazed at Melanie as an enigmatic smile played over his angular features. "I think the devil's advocate would probably be more accurate," he quipped.

They all greeted one another with special consideration being given to Lenore.

She appeared to be very pleased with their thoughtfulness; however, lines of stress were beginning to appear on her face.

"Dr. Books, do you have the results of Mac's tests?" Lenore inquired.

"Yes, I do, Lenore. The tests, I am sorry to say, revealed acute leukemia." The room was filled with a terrible silence as if everyone held their breath in shocked disbelief. He then continued. "However, with chemotherapy and with stem cell research that is being performed, there's every hope that he will go into remission and will be able to lead a relatively normal life. We have had much success in treating leukemia, but it is difficult to tell how he will respond at the outset."

Dr. Brooks turned to look at the rest of the family present and then suggested to them, "I would like all of you to think positively and be as cheerful and optimistic as possible each time that you come to visit Mac. His state of mind is a very important part of his therapy."

Lenore felt as if she had been unexpectedly struck. She was not prepared for such devastating news. Before his illness, she fully expected her husband to live a very long and full life. Mac always seemed so vigorous and healthy and continued to have a zest for life. How was Mac himself going to cope with this kind of news, she wondered. Lenore clutched at her umbrella with all her strength as she desperately held back the tears.

How well would she weather this stormy period? She simply had to be brave for her husband's sake.

Dr. Brooks once more turned to Lenore and said, "Mac, of course, knows nothing about his condition, but as soon as he becomes more responsive, I think that he should be told."

"Dad is a realist," Melanie interrupted. "He would never forgive us if we tried to keep this from him."

"Yes, I'm sure that's true," Dr. Brooks replied. "He has the right to know, and I'll explain everything to him as soon as it's feasible to do so. I'm going in now to see how he's doing. You can come in with me, Lenore."

As Lenore and Dr. Brooks walked into Mac's room, he seemed to stir and then slowly opened his eyes.

"Mac," Dr. Brooks said, "your wife is here to see you. Do you think that you could say hello to her?"

Mac looked at Lenore, making an attempt to say something. His lips formed the word hello, but no sound came out.

"That's wonderful, darling!" Lenore exclaimed. "Keep trying and I'm sure you'll be able to speak very soon." Lenore had to believe that what she said would actually become a reality. In the past, they had communicated well together, spending many hours in casual conversation or debating on a company policy. Now that his illness could very possibly take him away from her, Lenore needed some reassurance that, until that time, she would at least be able to converse with him again. But today, she was very grateful that he was able to show recognition.

"There is every hope that Mac will be able to speak very soon. He had a mild stroke with no evidence of paralysis. There is some weakness in his extremities, but that will improve with time. I assure you, Lenore, that within a few days, you'll see a change in your husband."

"I believe you, Dr. Brooks, but I'm simply a bit impatient." Lenore turned to look at Mac, who seemed to be somewhat more alert.

Mac understood everything that the doctor had said. He had fleeting moments when it was difficult to concentrate on conversations going on around him, but at the moment, this was not the case. He felt frustrated and resentful that he was being discussed as if he were not present. After all, he thought, it was his speech that seemed to be impaired, certainly not his mind. But as long as he was not able to speak, everyone would probably keep on treating him as a nonperson. The critical state of his illness was also making him less tolerant. Mac tried to speak again, but some inaudible sounds were all he could make.

Lenore took her husband's hand in an effort to calm him. "It's all right, Mac. It'll come back in time."

"I'll leave you two alone for a while," Dr. Brooks said and walked out of the room.

Dr. Paul Glasser practically collided with him as he walked past Mac's room. "Traffic is heavy around here!"

"Hey, Paul," Dr Brooks called out, "you're just the one I want to see. Have you met Mac Stone's granddaughter? She's a beauty!"

"No," replied Paul, "I haven't had the pleasure. Where is she?"

"Come with me." Dr. Brooks walked him over to the waiting room where Vanessa and her daughter, Marissa, sat and introduced Paul to them. "Paul is the ICU intern and is helping me to take care of Mac."

Dr. Paul Glasser was instantly drawn to Marissa. She appeared to be somewhat shy and sensitive and not as aggressive and outspoken as many of the nurses he was used to dating. To him, it was a refreshing change. Seizing the opportunity to get to know Marissa, he decided to ask her to accompany him to the coffee shop. When she accepted, he was very pleased. They had immediately found a common ground, and a sparkling conversation ensued as they walked together down the hall toward the elevators.

Chapter 4

A couple of hours had passed. The rain continued to match the grim reality of the unfolding day and all that had been revealed. It came down in rivulets on the windows, like tears streaming down with disappointment. Melanie and Vanessa sat in the waiting room, contemplating and discussing what had transpired earlier.

From out of the bustling hallway, Dr. Brooks walked into the waiting area with a couple of patients' charts in hand. "Are you two still sitting here with your long faces? I'm going to prescribe a smile for each one of you and some form of entertainment of your choice with unlimited refills, of course. It is to be taken as soon as possible."

Both women looked at him in amusement.

"Richard Brooks, you are a miracle worker," Melanie retorted. "Every time your pretty face appears, our problems seem to vanish."

"Melanie, you're only saying that because you want to take advantage of me."

"You're absolutely right. I have to be honest with you, I'm only interested in your brain."

"Personally, I think you're overlooking a very interesting body. I'm always being compromised by my female patients. In fact, I was once even compromised by a male patient. It's been very difficult trying to protect my virtue."

"I don't blame them," Melanie quipped. "If I were a patient here for any length of time, I'd probably jump at anything that moved."

Vanessa sat back somewhat reticent but still attentive and enjoying the conviviality of the conversation taking place. She was very fond of her sister-in-law, Melanie, and always enjoyed her company. Vanessa discretely wished that her husband, Greg, would have acquired some of his sister's good-natured humor.

Greg viewed life much more seriously than did his sister. His work took precedence over everything, including his wife and daughter. Lately, he appeared to be even more engrossed than ever before. If he was having problems, whether personal or business, he rarely discussed them with Vanessa. She surmised that, to Greg, an insurmountable problem was a sign of weakness that he could not express to his wife. Consequently, he would become inaccessible. Vanessa felt helpless in dealing with this kind of situation, especially when her husband's pride was at stake. But she kept her distance until he would reach some kind of resolve. She wanted to share in every aspect of his life, to be a worthy participant, whether it be in his business or personal life. To Vanessa, it was a constant source of frustration that she would never overcome.

The intensity of her subconscious mind seemed to suddenly bring forth the vision of her husband. For a moment, Vanessa thought that she was merely seeing an illusion in the doorway of the waiting room. But as he spoke, she was brought to the realization that her husband was actually there, in body and spirit, walking toward her.

"How's Dad doing today? Have all the tests been completed?" Greg asked as he approached his wife.

"Yes, Greg," Vanessa answered, "all the tests have been done. Your father's been asleep most of the afternoon. They must have exhausted him."

Greg then turned to Dr. Brooks, who seemed to be studying him. "By now you must have the results, Richard." Greg spoke with a hint of impatience apparent in his voice. He was used to prompt results in his passionate quest for perfection, which he expected from everyone, including himself.

Dr. Brooks reiterated to him what he had earlier divulged to the rest of the family. As he did so, Vanessa watched the color drain from her husband's face and the furrows in his brow deepen. Greg suddenly appeared older and almost haggard. "My God," he said somewhat tremulously, "acute leukemia! It can't be true. It's a mistake. The tests must not be accurate." He paused briefly to collect himself. "He's dying, isn't he?" Greg asked in a low voice.

"Don't give up on your father at the outset. Give him a fighting chance," Dr. Brooks replied. "He might just surprise you and live for a number of years. Greg, as I've said to the rest of your family, you must remain optimistic, and you must deal with Mac in the same manner. If you treat him as if he were a dying man, he will lose his desire to fight this illness. We must not have that, Greg."

"I understand, Richard. It's just that this entire thing has been so unexpected, and I need some time to adjust to the shock. After all, we are discussing my father's life. He happens to be a very important and vital man. Suddenly, he's been reduced to a mere shell of the man he had once been."

"Take it easy, dear brother," Melanie said. "I haven't seen you this emotional since your daughter, Marissa, was about to be born. Besides, the discovery of a cure could very well be imminent."

Melanie as well as Vanessa were amazed at Greg's anxiety. It was very unusual to see him in this condition. He always seemed to be in full control of his emotions. But then, no one so important to him had ever been so ill.

"Why don't we all pay Dad a short visit and then leave," Melanie suggested. "There's Mom, Marissa, and that intern, Dr. Glasser, coming out of Dad's room now. They look pretty cheerful, so things must be looking up."

"Mac was so pleased to see Marissa," Lenore exclaimed. "He seemed to be bubbling over with joy."

"He said a few words that were actually understandable," Marissa added very excitedly. "I'll bet that he'll be able to speak again very soon. What do you think, Paul?" She looked up at Dr. Glasser with trust and admiration. To her, his opinion was of paramount importance.

The intern, of course, was pleased, as well as flattered, that this lovely girl he had just met would hold so much esteem for him. "It certainly does seem very likely," Dr. Glasser replied, "since your grand father is making such an effort to regain his speech. I hope that he is able to speak very soon, for your sake as well as his own, Marissa."

Marissa was beaming with delight, directing a glowing smile toward Dr. Glasser.

Greg, Melanie, and Vanessa each took their turn visiting briefly with Mac. He was beginning to tire and shortly dropped off to sleep. Dr. Brooks walked into the room and suggested that Mac should have no more visitors tonight so that he could get some rest.

The next day, Mac was alert and was trying desperately to speak. He was finding that the more effort he put into his speech, the more words he was able to pronounce distinctly. He, along with the doctors, was also very pleased that his pneumonia had cleared up. It produced the optimistic hope that Dr. Brooks was waiting for, the proper frame of mind to break the news to him about his diagnosis.

Dr. Brooks examined Mac, keeping the conversation jovial. "You seem to be doing extremely well, Mac. Your heart has a good, strong beat. I'll bet that it's healthier than mine."

Mac tried to ask the doctor when he'd be able to speak properly again and was able to make himself understood. He was pleased with his own progress but felt impatient with his inability to converse smoothly and clearly.

"It'll come in time, Mac. I assure you of it. You seem to improve a little every day. Before long, you'll have your full speech capability regained. Right now, however, we do have a little problem that must be addressed."

Mac nodded with a questioning expression on his face. He wondered what more was in store for him. He had an overriding desire to be back to his strong and inimitable self once more. But he sensed that there was about to be another hurdle thrown in his path. The contest was not yet over.

Dr. Brooks continued. "At first, we thought that you were suffering from a minor blood dyscrasia, like some form of anemia. But further studies showed an overproduction of lymphocytes in your blood as well as in your bone marrow, Mac. The tests revealed acute leukemia." He hesitated a moment to observe Mac's reaction. The news appeared to be staggering to him. He looked distraught but did not try to speak.

Dr. Brooks went on. "We will begin with a course of deep X-ray therapy, and if necessary, we will give you chemotherapy. It may make you feel ill, but we can give you something to help relieve the nausea. You know, we've made great strides in combating leukemia, so there's every hope that you will go into remission and outlive us all"

Mac understood the magnitude of what he had just heard. He felt that this could very well be the beginning process to the end of his life. How ironic that he was in the business of saving and prolonging lives. That was the way he had always felt about his pharmaceutical company, which he had established so long ago. Now his life could be ebbing away and he could not take control of it. Mac finally spoke. "Ah . . . I too old to . . . outlive you. D—does ma wife kn—know?"

"Yes," replied Dr. Brooks, "she does know and intends to be very supportive. You're a very lucky man, Mac, to have such a devoted wife."

Mac nodded in agreement, and a smile played over his face. Lenore had always been loving and faithful to him, even during all of the difficult years of early adjustment. Mac was a fledgling then, just building up his business, which had been a mere fragment of what it is today. He had spent a great deal of time away from her and from his children. His new company was demanding and an enormous consumer of time. In addition, Mac had always aspired to greatness, and his company was a means to that end.

Mac's father, Jonathan Stone, was a pharmacist by profession and owned an apothecary. It was a modest business but one which earned for the family a generous clientele and kept them in the mainstream of society, such as existed in a small town. His mother had died giving birth to Mac, and as a result, his father had to find someone to care for the baby while he worked in the store. The child's grandmother took care of Mac till he was six. However, she died of a heart attack shortly after his sixth birthday, and Jonathan Stone was again looking for someone to care for his son.

Anastasia Kerensky was a lovely young Russian woman who had come to his store with a little boy of two. She needed a job and a place to live for herself and her little boy, Ivan.

Anastasia had been married to a Russian scientist, who sent his young wife and child to the United States just before the Bolshevik Revolution in 1917. Massive desertions, riots, and fighting between factions broke out, and a moderate socialist government under his cousin's rule was overthrown in a violent coup by the Bolsheviks.

Ivan's father was killed during the Bolsheviks' brutal oppression. He had planned to eventually defect to America but was never given the opportunity. Consequently, Anastasia and her son were left alone to fend for themselves in this country that was so new and foreign to them. Fortunately, Anastasia had learned the English language as a girl. Therefore, her husband felt that she would be able to survive whether he was able to eventually join her in America or not.

Jonathan Stone was immediately taken with this charming woman, who spoke with a Russian accent, and her wonderful little son. He hired her immediately as a governess to teach and to care for his six-year-old son, MacGregor, whom he called Mac.

The two boys played well together and learned much from Anastasia as well as from each other. Jonathan had given Anastasia and her son a large room on the second floor with an adjoining bath and never suggested that she do anything but care for his son, Mac. But because of his generosity and good nature, she felt a sense of obligation and a desire to do more for this small family. She demonstrated her culinary ability to Jonathan and also kept his home neat and spotless. Anastasia proved herself to be a very resourceful and intelligent young woman.

Jonathan was extremely pleased with her and felt that she was some kind of wonderful blessing that was given to him in return for his wife. After his wife had passed away, Jonathan thought that he would never love another woman. But now, he felt stirrings in him that he hadn't felt in many years.

Every evening, after Jonathan had closed the apothecary for the night, he looked forward to seeing Anastasia. He loved to observe her playing games with the boys. It was obvious that she enjoyed them, and they retuned her admiration and affection.

Jonathan decided that this particular evening was going to be a special one. He gathered up a few things to bring home, including a box of chocolate candy that he intended to present to Anastasia. That evening, he asked her to marry him, and she had joyfully accepted.

The wedding ceremony took place a month later in a lovely little white frame church just two blocks away from the store. The sun glimmered in the sky in celebration of the jubilant event. The church was filled with Jonathan's friends, who wished the couple well. Most of them spent many years trying to match him with every eligible female in town. He had not been interested in anyone and swore to them all that he would never marry again. When Anastasia came into his life, everything had changed for him. After all of those empty years, he found himself falling in love again. He finally stopped mourning his dead wife and looked forward to a new and glorious life. His love for Anastasia was a strong and powerful force, and he longed for this day when she would belong to him.

Anastasia looked lovely in her dress of pale blue crepe, which brought out the cornflower blue in her eyes. She wore her silky long, blond hair up in a loose bun held together with a spray of blue forget-me-nots and a cascade of blue ribbons.

Jonathan found his new wife breathtaking and was the envy of all of his male friends who had attended the wedding. A small reception after the ceremony was held in the garden behind Jonathan's home.

Mac and Ivan became stepbrothers and rejoiced in this new revelation. The idea of being suddenly related fascinated the boys since they had already enjoyed a mutual and close friendship. This camaraderie had continued throughout their youth and into adulthood.

In college, Mac majored in business and accounting, and Ivan had chosen chemistry as his major. He wanted to be a scientist as his late father had been. He also retained his name, Kerensky, in his father's memory.

After college, they each went their separate ways to gain experience in their own particular field. Mac eventually had saved enough money to invest in a small pharmaceutical company. His father then sold his small apothecary and joined forces with his son. The company became known as Stone Pharmaceutical Labs. After a few years, Ivan came to work there also as one of the lab's top scientists. The family was together once more, gathering strength and vitality from one another, with an enormous enthusiasm to succeed.

The company grew and prospered and continued to become larger and larger with each passing year. It had, indeed, proven to be a tremendously successful business venture. After all, they were dealing with the vehicles with which to sustain and improve life.

Drugs were always a necessity, so the demand for them flourished. Many new and better varieties were being discovered and were being marketed to help in the advancement of medical care. It was an exciting, as well as lucrative, business, and MacGregor Stone had finally realized greatness, wealth, and power.

Now, for the first time in his adult life, he had been reduced to this babbling and helpless old man. A simple request required Mac to make a profound effort in trying to speak and to be understood. Mac was losing patience with himself as well as the nursing staff. Communication would be much easier if he could write his requests and messages down and have them read rather than struggling to be understood. But, of course, the medical staff did not agree with his suggestion because he would then simply cease trying to improve his speech.

There, however, was something very critical that Mac wished to write, which was to be included with his will. He was trying desperately one morning to communicate to one of the nurses his need without divulging his very personal reason. "Baber eh ben . . . bease!" Mac kept repeating to the nurse who was giving him a bath. She was a robust woman with a rather masculine voice who would not break or bend any rules. She did not appear to possess a single vulnerable area in her character. It became a battle of the wills, but Mac persisted in his attempts to be accommodated.

"Sorry, Mac," she said, "you're going to have to do it the hard way. You'll learn to speak distinctly soon enough." As she completed her task of scrubbing Mac's body to the very bone, she turned on her heel and marched out of the room, still refusing to comply with his request.

Miserable old bat, thought Mac. *How did such an insensitive old fool become a nurse?* In anger, he reached for the emesis basin, which sat on the table near his bed, and flung it to the floor. The clattering could be heard down the hall all the way to the nurses' station.

Suddenly, at the entrance to his room appeared a very young nurse with an astonished expression on her face. "Are you having a problem, Mr. Stone?" She found the emesis basin on the floor in the far corner of the room and placed it back on the table.

Upon seeing the young girl, Mac felt that he was given a reprieve. This sweet girl will be easier to deal with, thought Mac. He made another attempt at verbalizing his request. "Baber eh ben," he muttered and simultaneously gestured with his hands to make himself comprehensible.

The young nurse regarded Mac and responded, "Did you say that you wanted paper and a pen, Mr. Stone? I'd be glad to get them for you."

Mac grinned broadly and kept nodding. What a wonderful girl, Mac thought. All of the nurses around here should be just like her. Life would be so much more pleasant.

When the nurse returned with some writing paper and a ballpoint pen, Mac was so grateful that he took the girl's hand and kissed it. She became flustered and giggled then walked quickly out of the room.

Mac took the paper and pen in hand and began writing, with some difficulty, the letter that he wished to include in his will.

Chapter 5

Several days went by and, quite frequently, Mac would become very ill due to the chemotherapy he was receiving. Eventually, the antinausea medication started to work, and he began to respond to the treatment. His speech had finally returned, and he was feeling stronger. Mac was now longing to be released from his entrapment, this rather small room with the unremitting four walls that held him hostage. Each time Dr. Brooks made his rounds, Mac would try to entice him into giving him a discharge.

"Consider this a vacation, Mac. Just relax and get plenty of rest," advised Dr. Brooks. "We have to see a complete reversal of your disease before we can consider sending you home. You may think that you're tough, and maybe you are, but until we have definite proof that you're in remission, we're keeping you right here."

"Okay, Doc, you win. I think you're tougher than I am right now, so I'll let you have your way."

"Did I hear right?" came a voice from the doorway. "Tough Mac Stone is going to succumb to the doctor's wishes." Ivan Kerensky overheard part of the conversation as he walked into Mac's room.

"Ivan, it's so good to see you," Mac said. "How are things progressing at the lab?"

"Everything seems to be under control, but everyone misses you, of course."

"That's what I like to hear. It makes me feel almost immortal." He then turned to look at Dr. Brooks. "Richard, this is my stepbrother, Ivan Kerensky. He's in charge of our scientific research department, a genius in his field."

"Pleased to meet you, Mr. Kerensky," Dr. Brooks replied. "That's quite a testimony to you. You two must be very close. I hope you will be a good influence on Mac. He seems to be eager to leave the hospital and get into the mainstream of things. But I assure you, it's much too early."

"I will do my best," Ivan replied. "However, I do have a business matter which I must discuss with Mac. I'll try not to take up much of his time."

"Then I'll leave you two alone so that you can have some privacy. It was a pleasure meeting you, Mr. Kerensky."

"The feeling is mutual, Dr. Brooks," Ivan answered.

Richard Brooks walked out of the room. He jotted some notes in Mac's chart at the nurses' station and then left the hospital for his office. It was located just a short distance from the hospital in a large medical building that was occupied by a variety of medical professionals. The range of specialties spanned every aspect of the human anatomy.

Dr. Brooks was an internist and had a well-established practice with a tremendous log of patients. Therefore, he was kept very busy, tending to his patients' needs, those who visited his office as well as the ones, like Mac, who were admitted to the hospital. This, of course, allowed him very little time for his personal life, which, presently, was almost nonexistent.

His wife divorced Richard after just a few short years of marriage due mostly to loneliness. She wanted a husband who would spend a great deal of time with her. Unfortunately, Richard was a victim of his profession as well as his dedication to his patients. His wife, being very young, was not able to deal with this and often said that his practice was his mistress and was beyond challenging.

After she left, Richard felt terribly responsible and guilt-ridden because he had let her down. At that point in his life, he made a decision never to marry again. He felt that he could not do justice to his profession as well as a wife and a family. At first, he spent numerous disconsolate hours alone at home or would occasionally remain in his office, dropping off to sleep on a sofa. Eventually, he began to date and found that he preferred his freedom over being married. He was now devoting as much time as he chose to his work and felt no pressure as he did while he was married. Richard's life was now stabilized to his own satisfaction.

Of course, he realized that every lifestyle had its drawbacks. The marital state meant responsibility to and for another human being and also meant love and companionship whenever he wanted and needed it. The single state meant freedom and responsibility for himself alone, not having to answer to anyone else, and being his own man. Presently, this seemed to be of great importance and a totally consuming need. It also meant occasional loneliness, but he was generally able to handle it well.

As Richard proceeded toward his office building, he noticed Melanie Lambert walking from the parking lot toward the hospital. "Melanie," he called, and she turned to see his familiar face. He walked over to her and said, "Melanie, you look lovely and well rested today."

"Why, thank you, Richard. That's a terrific compliment to hear the first thing in the morning. How's my dad doing today?"

"He's holding his own. In fact, he's doing better than that. I'm very pleased with his progress. But I don't think that you should visit him right now."

"Oh, is he asleep?"

"No, but he had a visitor as I left him, his stepbrother, Ivan. He said that he had some business to discuss with your father but that it wouldn't take long. So I allowed it. Your father seems quite eager to get back in the swing of things."

"I wonder what Uncle Ivan wanted to discuss with Dad that couldn't wait. He could take it up with Greg instead."

"Don't let it worry your pretty head, Melanie. Come on, walk me to my office. I have about an hour before my patients begin pouring into my waiting room."

"Well, I suppose I could do that," Melanie replied with some hesitation.

"Don't look at me like that, Melanie. All I'm going to do is make a few passes at you," Richard chided with a guileless open grin.

Melanie let out a giggle, which prompted her to feel that she had digressed for the moment. She took his arm and said, "Well then, let's get going. I can hardly wait!"

"Great!" Richard exclaimed, continuing the animation. "Let's get out of this hot sun and into the privacy of my shady air-conditioned office."

"Well," Melanie teased, "that certainly does sound rather shady."

They walked arm in arm till they reached Richard's office.

The day showed promise of being warm and sunny, the kind of day that warmed the very soul. The sky was a penetrating blue and was streaked with contrasts of a few gleaming white clouds.

Inside the medical offices of Dr. Richard Brooks sat two figures drinking coffee and in the midst of an engrossing conversation on a large leather sofa. They faced large casement windows from which hung baskets of fern, grape ivy, and coleus. In a large container standing on the floor in the corner to the right of the windows was clump of *Ficus benjamina* completing the spectacle. One of Richard's hobbies was growing and propagating plants.

Melanie shared his enthusiasm for plants and, upon entering his office, expressed great admiration for his rather breathtaking diorama of greenery.

His source of great pride was his accomplishment with the Japanese art of bonsai, which was lavishly displayed on his desk.

"Oh, Richard," Melanie exclaimed as she approached the desk, "I love what you've done with this bonsai plant. I've seen very few specimens that can compare with this one. You certainly are talented."

"Being the art critic that you are, Melanie, I consider it quite a compliment." Richard had admired her ever since he had seen her that evening at her brother's home a few years ago.

It was at a New Year's Eve party at the home of Greg and Vanessa Stone where Melanie made a lasting impression upon him. Richard had arrived early, before any of the other guests. This was the first party he had attended since his divorce. He came alone and was feeling rather conspicuous and uncomfortable, but Greg insisted that it was time for him to begin to mingle.

Greg and Richard were friends for most of their lives, and they were always completely honest with each other. Greg felt that Richard's choice of wife had shown poor judgment on his part and that he was merely fascinated by her youth and attractiveness, but for the most part, he felt that she was not suitable to be a doctor's wife. She proved him to be correct within a relatively short time, expressing much immaturity and self-indulgence.

While he was just establishing his practice, Richard would spend many long hours with his patients, especially those who were hospitalized. He would arrive at home late and would then be subjected to her anger. Then an intolerable silence between them lasted for days. She would upset him emotionally to the point where it was affecting his work. When she finally left, it was somewhat of a relief yet, simultaneously, a source of heartbreak for him. He felt partially to blame but did not know what else he could have done to remedy the situation while it lasted. His career was of great importance to him, and he refused to abandon it. He expected his wife to be more tolerant of his erratic schedule since they would both profit by it once he was established. Unfortunately, she lacked the perseverance that this kind of life required.

Melanie and Alan Lambert had also been invited to the party at Greg's home. Several other couples had attended the party as well as a few who came alone, as did Richard.

He began a conversation with Melanie as they reached for the same hors d'oeuvre at the refreshment table. "It looks like we'll have to fight over it." Richard picked up a container of cocktail toothpicks and handed them to Melanie. "Lady, choose your weapon."

"Personally, I'd prefer to break it in half rather than duel over it," Melanie retorted. She separated the cracker with the caviar into two sections and affectionately fed one of the sections into Richard's mouth. "I'm Melanie Lambert, Greg's younger sister."

"Of course, Melanie, it's good to see you again. I'm Richard Brooks. You have excellent taste in hors d'oeuvres."

"Why, thank you, Richard. You're my brother's friend, the doctor."

"Yes, that's right. Your memory serves you well."

Melanie eyed the table again. "How would you like to split a swedish meatball with me?"

"I will if you'll let me do the honor." Richard put a small piece of the meatball on a dish, broke it with a fork, and lifted a section to Melanie's mouth. Through the entire evening, he did not miss an opportunity to tease her.

Richard had only a vague recollection of Melanie as his friend's younger sister, but she had changed a great deal since they were in college. All traces of her shyness were gone, and she was much lovelier than he had envisioned.

Alan had spent the evening in lengthy legal discussion with a couple of other guests. At many social gatherings such as this, he would make an effort to converse with every guest present in anticipation of establishing new clientele.

Richard had asked Melanie to dance just before the stroke of midnight. While everyone was busy exchanging New Year's wishes, Richard made it a point to give Melanie a warm New Year's kiss on the cheek as they danced to "Auld Lang Syne." She responded to him and then felt some embarrassment. However, he had never forgotten that moment.

Being with her now, alone in his office, had reminded him of that New Year's Eve and how much he had enjoyed her company. A few years had passed since that party. During that time, he had not seen her until her father became ill.

"We have a lot of catching up to do," Melanie said, suddenly breaking the moment of silence. "I haven't seen you in years. What have you been up to, besides spending a lot of time in your foliated Xanadu?"

"I guess most of my time is spent working. Occasionally, I play golf and tennis and in the winter, I sometimes take a couple of weeks off for skiing, either in Aspen or somewhere else."

"Seems like you're enjoying your life these days, doing everything you want. Do you ever get lonely?"

"Yes and no," Richard replied. "I do have a lot of freedom, but the nights can sometimes get very long and lonely."

"Have you kept up your friendship with my brother, Greg, and his wife, Vanessa?"

"I've seen them from time to time, both socially and professionally. They are my patients, you know, just as are your parents."

"That's right. I've forgotten about that." She looked up at him and read in the gleam of his eyes what his mind was thinking. "And now you think it's my turn. You'd like to give me a physical."

Richard smiled at her mischievously. "What makes you think I haven't already given you one?"

"You haven't changed at all, Richard. You've always been a little corrupt. Seriously though, seeing you again like this makes me reminiscent of the past."

"Yes, I'm feeling the same, Melanie. It's good to see you again and to have this opportunity to talk." He scrutinized her for a moment, weighing his thoughts. "And how is your husband, Alan, doing?"

"He's doing very well. His success is keeping him busy much of the time. We would have made plans to get away for a while, but since Dad became ill, we decided to forego them for now."

"You certainly are a good daughter, Melanie. That's very thoughtful of you."

"That's what my mother has been saying to me. I don't consider myself particularly unusual. It's just the natural thing to do when one's parent becomes ill. After all, they have always taken good care of me. Now, I feel that it's my turn to reciprocate."

Richard watched her closely as he continued to probe. "Does Alan take good care of you too, Melanie? Does he always make you happy?"

"Yes, we've been happy. I would prefer to see him more often, but he does have a lot of responsibilities and pressures at work. In order to remain successful, he has to devote a great deal of time to his job. He is good at it, and I am proud of him. I wouldn't have him any other way."

"You know, Melanie, that's the very speech I would have loved to hear from someone else who had meant so much to me a long time ago. Unfortunately, all I ever heard were constant demands and criticisms until the pressure became too intense. Since we've parted and gone our separate ways, I've had some regrets. But more importantly, I have felt a sense of relief. Alan is a lucky guy to have found such a terrific lady. I hope that he realizes what a gem he has in you."

"Quit patronizing me, Richard. It's embarrassing."

But Richard continued unrelentingly. "Before any of us were married, I should have dated you, but the problem was that you were my best friend's little sister, and I simply couldn't see beyond that. I visualized you merely as a cute kid, someone who was fun to tease, that's all."

"Since this seems to be the time for past revelations," Melanie confided, "I must tell you this, even though I don't know what purpose it will serve. I used to have an enormous crush on you in those days.

But knowing that you never took me seriously, I didn't want you to know how I felt. So I kept it a secret."

"And what about now?" Richard asked as the buzzer on his desk summoned him.

"Ah, saved by the buzzer!" Melanie said with a sigh of relief. "If you don't start calling in your patients soon, they'll be using four-letter words to describe you, as they sit impatiently in your waiting room."

"Okay, Melanie, you win. We'll continue this discussion another time. See you later." He watched her wistfully as she walked out of his office and then answered his intercom.

* * *

Ivan Kerensky was just concluding his conversation with Mac in his hospital room.

"Please, Ivan," Mac said, "do as I ask. I have very good reason to do this. It is my privilege to make that choice."

"I don't agree, but I'll comply with your wishes, Mac," Ivan said with much reluctance. "You always were a stubborn man. I've always had so much love and respect for you as if you were my blood brother. But I do feel that you are not using good judgment now. In fact, you're not in a position to make wise decisions of any kind right now. Can't you see that, Mac?"

"I appreciate your concern, Ivan, but I cannot, and will not, change my mind. Whether you believe it or not, I am in full control of all of my faculties. I am able to make proper decisions, even from a hospital bed."

"All right, Mac. I'll be leaving now. If you should come to your senses and change your mind, please give me a call. You can be sure, Mac, that I'll be praying you will. Good-bye, dear brother."

Ivan looked very depressed as he walked out of Mac's room. He was deeply engrossed in thought and did not realize that he was being observed by Dr. Paul Glasser.

Feeling some consternation, Dr. Glasser decided to find out what had transpired in Mac's room. As Ivan walked past, Dr. Glasser obstructed his way. "Excuse me, sir. I noticed that you just came from Mac Stone's room. Is there anything wrong? You seem very upset."

"No, Doctor, Mac and I had a serious discussion dealing with business. He, unfortunately, made a decision which I feel was a poor one, based on pure emotion. Important decisions should be based on logic, certainly not emotion. He's fine, if you are concerned, but he's as stubborn as ever. I'm his stepbrother, Ivan Kerensky, and have known him for most of my life. Therefore, I'm well aware that when Mac comes to a decision, he sticks to it no matter what. My worry is that he's too ill to make a wise one, but of course, he insisted that he was fully capable."

"Well, Mr. Kerensky, he's been progressing very nicely, and I would tend to agree with Mr. Stone. I'd better check on him, in case your conversation was a bit more than he was able to handle. Thank you, sir. It was a pleasure meeting you." Paul Glasser extended his hand to Ivan in a warm handshake. He then proceeded to Mac's room.

Mac was sitting up on the bed with an impervious expression on his face. He did not notice when Dr. Glasser walked into the room.

"Mac," he said, "is there something troubling you? You seem very deeply lost in your thoughts. Is there anything you'd like to share with me? I'd like to help if I can."

"You are helping me by the mere fact that you are concerned. And medically, you are an excellent and, I must say, dedicated intern. You don't often run into someone with such commendable qualities in their youth. It takes a lot of discipline to become a good physician. So many young people allow too many distractions to be able to devote all their energies to one purpose."

"Well, sir, I do my best, and I happen to like what I do. The most difficult part has been the lack of money and, of course, being on call during the night with an emergency taking place. Having to drag myself out of bed when I've been in a deep sleep is really hell. But that doesn't happen too often."

Mac showed some amusement at the young intern's candid comments. He reminded Mac of his own son, Greg, when he was approximately twenty years younger and being primed for his business.

He longed for that time when he had so many years to look forward to and life still held so much promise for him. If he hadn't become ill, he might have lived for quite some time. But now, he was grateful for each day that passed. If only, he thought, his body had not succumbed to the dreadful disease that was slowly and silently encroaching upon him.

Dr. Glasser noted the sudden languidness that began to sweep over Mac's face. "Come on, Mac, cheer up. You're doing just fine, you know."

"I know. I know. I just feel a little sleepy right now. Maybe I'll take a short nap before my wife comes to visit me."

"That's a good idea, Mac. I'll leave you alone and tend to the rest of my patients."

After Dr. Glasser left, Mac settled in and fell asleep. However, he had a rather fitful sleep, full of fragmentary dreams of his demise. To him, life had become something fleeting and elusive. He no longer made plans for the future, and consequently, his dreams were filled with dread, yet with some resolve.

In a constant and recurring dream, he could see his family being torn away from him one at a time by gusts of wind that came in great waves. He tried desperately to hold on to every last one of them, but it was to no avail. The very last one was Lenore, his beloved wife, whom he held on to with such ferocity that it caused pain to radiate through his arm, rendering it useless. He was forced to let go. He then envisioned himself standing completely alone and abandoned in an immense and boundless field, interrupted only by images and personifications of death. And it was rightfully so, for in death, he would take the journey alone.

While he slept, one of the hospital maintenance men came into Mac's room to check on his phone that was on his nightstand. Everything seemed to be just as he had intended, so he left the sleeping Mac.

Lenore passed the maintenance man leaving Mac's room and almost collided with him as she entered the room. "You startled me," she said. He simply nodded and walked away. Lenore stood by Mac's hospital bed and tried to wake him. He compulsively grabbed at her arm, almost wrenching it at the wrist, but he was not able to come out of his deep, almost comatose, sleep. He began to call her name and started to thrash about. Then, finally, he laid back quietly in complete exhaustion.

Lenore sat down in a chair next to Mac's bed and resolved to patiently wait till her husband was ready to awake on his own. He was obviously in much need of rest, and consequently, his body willed him to sleep. Pulling out a paperback novel from her tote bag, Lenore began to indulge herself in reading to pass the time and make the waiting period more bearable. Lately, she found herself doing this quite often.

Chapter 6

At Stone Pharmaceutical Labs, Greg was busily setting the wheels in motion to expand the company on European soil. He had received an unexpected positive reply from the board of directors when he had requested to do so. Still finding it difficult to believe his overwhelming good luck, Greg was tremendously elated this morning as he went through the mechanics of the necessary details. Overexpansion was risky. In the past, the board had followed the conservative leadership of his father. Mac seemed quite satisfied in keeping the company at its present size and located primarily in the United States and Canada. But this was true only of the past few years. In Mac's earlier, more progressive days, the company seemed to grow by leaps and bounds. Greg was eager to rekindle that spark of vitality once more in the company. Greg also felt the desire for some kind of significant and meaningful change. Prior to this, he was feeling stifled and stunted. He needed new challenges in his life. This new growth that he had planned for the company, Greg saw as a vehicle to that end. And he would pursue this for he knew that it would benefit him personally as well as financially. To him, wealth and power were synonymous. His desire was to make this enormous contribution something he engineered and guided of his own volition and not necessarily with his father's approval. It had to be a concept that originated through him and him alone, and now he had that opportunity.

His cell phone suddenly summoned him back to the present and out of his engrossing introspection. Greg answered it and found it was his sister, Melanie, on the phone.

"Hello, Melanie," he said, "how are you today?" Greg felt exhilarated due to the direction he had chosen and how bright his future appeared with that decision.

"I'm fine, Greg," Melanie answered with some anxiety apparent in her voice. "The reason I called was to let you know of an incident that occurred this morning. It has upset me and has also made me a bit curious."

"What is it, Melanie? Where are you?"

"I'm calling from the hospital, and I've just spoken with Dr. Glasser, who told me that Uncle Ivan visited with Dad for quite some time today, and he was a little worried that Dad might be taking on some business matters a little too soon. He should not have to worry about any business decisions at this time. He needs a great deal of rest. Have you any idea what they might have been discussing?"

"No, but Uncle Ivan and Dad have been up to something for quite some time now. They've been rather secretive about it too. On many occasions, I questioned Dad about what was going on between them, but he would always be very evasive. So I felt that it had nothing to do with business. Otherwise, I would have been in on the discussion." Greg paused for a moment and leaned forward in his chair. "I noticed that Alan joined them on a few occasions. Being the company lawyer, I couldn't help but feel that there had to be some kind of connection. Of course, I could be completely wrong. Why don't you try to get some answers from Alan tonight, Melanie?"

"I'll see what I can do, Greg. There's obviously something cooking because Alan did tell me that he had a meeting with Dad but would not let on what the conversation was about. If it is a business matter, you shouldn't be kept in the dark. After all, isn't the president of the company entitled to know everything that goes on within that company?"

"Well, you would certainly think so," Greg replied cynically but with some consternation. But then, he too was guilty of some rather conspiratorial behavior as well—his not consulting with Mac about his latest move toward enlarging the company. Because of this, Greg's visits to the hospital to see his father had been occasional and brief. He did not wish to divulge his plan since he was certain that his father would disapprove. But then, Mac was no longer chairman of the board. In his place, the interim chairman, David Warner, was much more attuned to progress.

"Have you approached Ivan about this?" Melanie pressed, trying to get to the bottom of the mystery.

"Yes, I have," Greg answered, "many times, but I've never been able to find out anything substantial."

"I've also learned today," Melanie continued, "that after Uncle Ivan left, Dad had been doing an awful lot of sleeping. Whatever he and Uncle Ivan were discussing seemed to have been very exhausting for Dad. He was having bad dreams as well. Every time he mumbled something incoherently or called Mom's name, she tried to wake him, but he simply continued to sleep."

"That does seem rather strange, doesn't it?" Greg probed around in his mind, attempting to arrive at a logical conclusion. "It appears to me that his sleeping is helping him to deal with something, and he's coming to terms with whatever it is that's bothering him."

"All right, Greg, I'll buy that bit of psychology. I hope it's accurate. Only time will tell. Well, you had better get back to work, and I'll get back to see if there is any change in Dad."

After completing his conversation, Greg walked out of his office determined to get some information on what might be going on between his father and Ivan. Was Alan involved too? As he walked down the hall toward the elevators, Renée Bordeaux caught sight of him coming from the opposite direction.

"How nice it is to see you again, Monsieur Stone. You seem very troubled. Is there any way that I can help?"

Greg paused for a moment, deciding whether or not to confide in Renée about his problem. Feeling that it would be pointless, he said, "No, I really don't think you can help me, Renée. If I change my mind, I'll let you know."

"You look as if you could use some cheering up. How would you like to join me for lunch? I know of a lovely restaurant about ten minutes from here which has a marvelous salad bar."

"There's something important that I must look into right now, and I am in a hurry, so you'll have to excuse me. I'll let you know about lunch a little later, Renée."

"I'll be waiting for your answer," Renée replied.

Greg excused himself and quickly took the elevator to another floor. He got off and walked to an office that was just a short distance away. The name on the door read Ivan Kerensky. In the outer office, Ivan's secretary sat at her desk as Greg walked in.

"Is Ivan in his office? I'd like, very much, to speak with him."

"I'm sorry, Mr. Stone," the secretary responded, "Mr. Kerensky was here for only a very short time today. Mr. Lambert came to see him, and they both left together just about fifteen minutes ago."

"Did they say where they were going?" Greg inquired. "Yes, sir, they were going to lunch, but I don't know where."

"Will you tell Ivan to get in touch with me when he gets back? Never mind, I'll call his cell instead."

"Certainly, Mr. Stone."

Greg walked out of the office filled with apprehension, wondering what was going on behind his back. Could he simply be overreacting? Could he be imagining this, or was there enough evidence to give him reason to suspect something? He decided to call Renée and meet her for lunch. She might be able to give him an insight as to what she had observed. He hoped to get to the bottom of this mystery in short order.

Greg and Renée sat at a corner table, enjoying their large leafy salads in an atmosphere of soft lights and music.

"Do you find this restaurant as enchanting as I do, Monsieur Stone?" Renée asked as she tasted the dressing on her salad.

"Yes, it is very charming, and the food is good, especially the salad bar. It's really exceptional." He paused for a moment, still looking at her and then with a grin said, "Renée, since this is our second lunch together, I really think that you could call me Greg, at least outside of the office."

"If you feel it is proper to call the president of the company by his first name, then it would give me great pleasure to do so, Greg." She returned his smile, and their eyes lingered together in a bond of friendship.

"You appear to be extremely happy today," Greg observed. "Is there any special reason for all of this elation?"

"Yes, Greg, there most certainly is." Out of sheer necessity, Renée told Greg of her most recent victory. "This is a celebration we are having. The Reynolds account is ours! Here is the document stating that we will be working with them." She took out a large Manila envelope and pulled out its contents. Renée had been bursting with delight ever since yesterday evening, when she learned that Stone Labs had the contract.

Greg skimmed through the papers that had been presented before him. "You are the best, Renée! You've done a terrific job, and you certainly are an asset to the company. This is a very large account. You just may be in for a promotion, young lady."

"Why, Greg, how generous of you. It was not that difficult for me to acquire it. Mr. Reynolds' assistant, Tom Rider, seemed to enjoy my company. He had asked me to dinner on a few occasions. We got along very well. Last evening, while we were having cocktails, he gave me the good news."

"I'm not at all surprised that he liked you, Renée. After all, there is nothing to dislike about you."

Her face illuminated with pleasure, and she smiled at him rather demurely. "Do you know what would give me the greatest pleasure?"

"No, Renée. What is that?"

"I would love to work directly with you as your assistant."

"I don't think I'd get any work done if you were my assistant," Greg replied with much amusement.

Suddenly, Greg noticed three men get up and proceed toward the door. They were Ivan, Alan, and a man he did not recognize.

Noticing the sudden change of expression on his face, Renée asked, "Is something wrong, Greg?" She turned to see the three men who Greg seemed to be watching. "Oh, Mr. Kerensky, Mr. Lambert, and that must be the gentleman they were meeting from the New England Cancer Institute."

Greg looked very puzzled. "He doesn't look familiar to me. Do you know his name?"

"No, I'm sorry, Greg, I don't, but I did overhear Mr. Lambert saying to Mr. Kerensky that they had to meet with the man from the cancer institute in ten minutes, and then they left the office. That was all I heard. I wish I could be of more help to you, Greg. You look so troubled."

"Just keep your beautiful eyes and ears open. Something seems to be going on behind the scenes, and I'm not being let in on the action."

"Don't you have any idea what has been going on?"

"No, there was nothing that I could actually put my finger on, until just recently. Well, I'm going to speak to Ivan as soon as I get back. I've left a message with his secretary and on his cell phone to call me."

"Well then, Greg, I'm sure that everything will be cleared up for you very soon. Now please enjoy your lunch."

"I'm sorry, Renée. It isn't fair to burden you with my problem. You asked me to lunch to celebrate your success. Why don't you tell me more about yourself? Your French accent is such a fascination to me."

Renée was extremely pleased by Greg's compliment. She enjoyed his company and did not mind discussing business or whatever he enjoyed. He possessed every quality that she found admirable in a man. She felt the desire to pursue him no matter what the consequences might be. She found him to be rather conventional with a very definite set of principles by which he lived. These qualities were very commendable but could prove to be quite a challenge to Renée.

She did not know Greg's wife very well and preferred it that way. In fact, she wished that she had never met Vanessa Stone. From brief observations, Vanessa appeared to be very sedate and almost prudish, she thought. Of course, that was only her opinion. She seemed attractive enough for her age, but someone younger and more vital would be more compatible with a man such as Greg. After all, he was absolutely magnificent. Renée then envisioned herself with Greg, living with him, loving him, and making love with him with glorious passion. She felt that she was perfect for him, a bit flamboyant perhaps but not overly so, just enough to make an interesting combination. Renée knew Greg found her attractive. His reaction to her proved this to be true.

Their remaining lunch hour was very pleasant, filled with sharing of excerpts from their lives. Renée secretly wished that time would stand still for them, that this precious moment could last forever, but of course, this could not be. Time had to progress, as it always did, in its usual fashion, and then the magic was gone.

Chapter 7

Shortly after they had returned to the offices of Stone Pharmaceutical Labs, Greg received a call from Ivan Kerensky. "Greg, I heard that you were looking for me earlier. What did you wish to discuss with me?"

"I spoke with Melanie earlier today, and she mentioned that you visited with Dad. How is he doing?"

"Oh, Greg, he's doing very well. Don't worry about him. He even seems eager to get back to work."

"But you aren't bringing business problems to him already, are you, Ivan?" There was some hesitation, and then Ivan spoke. It was partially a business matter and also personal in nature." Again, there was more hesitation. "I simply brought Mac up to date on what he has been missing at the lab, that's all. This illness is making your father feel very expendable and useless. He needs to keep his mind working and active. His work has kept him alert, and if he doesn't get back to it, he will stagnate. That wouldn't be good for his morale, I'm afraid."

"I hope that your discussion didn't tire him out." Greg was hedging, trying to gain more information. "Melanie mentioned that he seemed exhausted and had spent a lot of time sleeping."

"He didn't seem to be exhausted as I was leaving. In fact, he appeared to be very alert."

Greg was feeling the impatience souring within him. He wanted to explode with accusation and penetrate the mind of this inviolable person. But there was nothing to substantiate his suspicions. "I saw Alan here today. Is he still in the building?"

"No, he left after our luncheon." Ivan was not revealing anything. Greg continued with the inquest. "He didn't stop by my office at all. Did he have anything important on his mind?"

"No, Greg, we were discussing some minor details that needed to be ironed out. We managed just fine. It wasn't necessary to bother you."

"Okay, Ivan, I'm glad you did handle it."

"Is there anything troubling you, Greg? You seem a bit upset."

"No, Ivan, I don't suppose there is." Greg wondered at that point if he was being unusually suspicious until he heard more from Melanie. If she doesn't come up with something, he thought, *then I'll give the whole thing up.*

That evening, Alan and Melanie Lambert were having dinner in their beautiful suburban home with their twin boys, Mark and Derek. The conversation spanned the usual topics, from sports and schoolwork to the appeal and dislike of the various dishes that were on the table. Within a relatively short time, the boys had finished eating and were off to their respective rooms. Melanie had felt rather anxious during dinner, hoping for an opportunity of a conversation with Alan. The boys gave her that option by not lingering after they had finished eating their dessert. Melanie was very grateful for that.

"So, Alan, did you have an interesting day today? Did anything exciting happen?"

He looked up at her over his coffee. "Exciting? Well, let me think about that." He decided to toy with her. "On my way to work this morning, a huge tractor trailer overturned in front of me, so I put the accelerator to the floor and literally flew right over it. Then in the elevator at the office, two girls walked on with me and began disrobing as soon as the doors were closed. They then started pulling off my clothes, trying to get it on with me."

Melanie gave her husband a look of disgust and then broke into a wide grin. "Alan, you're out of your mind."

"Why can't you just tell me how imaginative and clever I am! That would be much kinder."

"I would if I thought you deserved it. Tell me, Alan, after experiencing so much in just one morning, were you brave enough to attempt going out to lunch?"

"Yes, as a matter of fact, I went to lunch with Ivan and Dan Ulrich from the New England Cancer Research Institute."

"Did Uncle Ivan say why he came to visit Dad today? Was it a business matter they were discussing? He really shouldn't burden Dad with anything just yet. He left Dad absolutely exhausted."

"Honey, Ivan doesn't tell me everything, you know." Alan looked a bit annoyed at the line of questioning and began to hurry with his coffee. Melanie refused to give up on the subject until she was sufficiently satisfied.

"Who is this Dan Ulrich?"

"You don't know him, Melanie. He's someone I knew a long time ago. Just recently, he contacted me again. Our conversation was mostly about business. You wouldn't be interested in the details."

"That's a typical male response." Melanie was becoming indignant. "The name isn't familiar to me. You must not have mentioned him before."

"What difference does it make if I forgot to mention him? We've had luncheon meetings together before. It's not unusual for me to have lunch with a client." There was some irritation apparent in his voice. He was attempting to dissipate his wife's curiosity, but it would not be appeased. He then pushed back his chair and began to stand up.

Melanie, still not finished questioning her husband, made an attempt to stop him from leaving the dining table. "There's something else I wanted to ask you, Alan. Have you been bringing business problems to Dad at the hospital?"

"Melanie, what is it with you tonight? Are you having me watched?"

"The hospital is a very public place, and the hospital staff sees everyone who comes and goes. You were visiting with Dad. Don't you see, Alan, Dad isn't really strong enough to cope with problems at the lab. It seems to me that Greg should be able to take care of things just fine. Why don't you consult with him instead?"

"Because, Melanie, my darling, the matter had to do with your father's last will and testament. I'm not at liberty to tell you any more than that. In fact, I myself don't know what it's all about. He handed me an envelope which was to be included in his will. He specified that it is not to be opened until his demise. He instructed me to give it to Greg for opening at that time. Now will you allow me to leave the table and read the newspaper peacefully?"

Feeling somewhat appeased, Melanie relinquished the questioning. "Yes, go ahead, Alan. I'm sorry, but you know how important open communication is to me."

"Yes, honey, I know." Alan walked up to her. He took her head in his hands and kissed her gently on the mouth. "You've never put me through such rigorous questioning before. You'd think I had gone to lunch with another woman."

"I almost wish you had. Then I would know the enemy, and I would know how to deal with her." This unknown entity was difficult to perceive. She could merely guess at what was actually happening, if anything at all. But she knew her husband to always be open and honest with her. That is what made their marriage work. Now, suspecting that her husband was hiding something from her, Melanie felt anxious.

As she cleared the table, Melanie watched Alan as he walked out of the dining room. She hoped that this was just a figment of her emotional state and was merely jumping to conclusions that were unfounded. Unfortunately, there was an uneasy feeling gnawing at her that was making her ill, and it would not pass. After Melanie had put the dirty dishes into the dishwasher, she sought out her husband. Alan was sitting, reading the evening newspaper, on a sofa near the fireplace in the next room. She sat down next to him and took a section of the paper. But her subconscious mind would not allow her to concentrate on the words in front of her.

Through his peripheral vision, Alan noticed his wife's apparent agitation. He put his arm around her with an embellishment of affection. "I didn't mean to be so abrupt with you, honey. It's just not like you to mistrust me so much."

"Alan, you've never given me reason to mistrust you before, not that there is any real basis now. It's just a feeling I have that won't go away."

"Well, I don't know what I can do about that. You'll simply have to work it out for yourself." Alan took the newspaper away from her and put it on the nearby table. He took her chin and gently turned her head to face him. "Let's not argue. Let's go upstairs instead and make love." He kissed her squarely on the mouth, and she submitted to him.

The following morning, as Alan was shaving, Melanie sat up in bed and observed him from a distance. Alan began to feel a bit uneasy from all of this scrutinizing. He was finding it difficult to function properly and, in fact, cut his face rather severely in the process while shaving. "Look, Melanie, I don't like this! It's making me uptight. My day is going to be disastrous." "I'm sorry, Alan. I was just thinking back to our conversation last evening."

"Okay, what is it this time, Melanie? What were you going to ask me?"

Well, I was wondering about this Dan Ulrich you mentioned. How did you meet him, Alan?"

Alan decided to relent and give Melanie more information. Otherwise, she would never ease her questioning. "As I told you before, he's someone I knew years ago. He had our firm represent him in a malpractice suit, which, unfortunately, we lost. As a result, he practically lost everything, including his self-esteem. I was the one who did the research, and Trent was his defense in court. I feel we should have won. However, the judge and jury were sympathetic with the plaintiff, who happened to be a young girl in her teens. It was discovered that she had a malignant growth on her jaw bone. Dan Ulrich was the surgeon who removed the tumor and her maxillary bone. The girl's parents felt that he performed a surgical procedure which was too radical and got another surgeon to back them up. Dan claimed he did only that which was necessary to save the girl's life. The malignant tumor had already invaded the bone. However, even with reconstructive surgery, she was somewhat deformed. Much later, I heard that the surgeon who testified against Dan was a friend of the girl's family. So in reality, Dan was really screwed."

"What a dreadfully sad story, Alan," Melanie replied after listening to her husband's narrative. She couldn't decide for whom she had more compassion, the poor girl who would probably spend the rest of her life deformed or the doctor whose career had been ruined. "My God. She then continued, "life must have been positively devastating for them both since then."

"Yes, I'm sure that it has been for the girl. But Dan has been working persistently at rebuilding his. He left the country for a while, but since his return, he's been doing a lot of research with anticancer drugs, and he has had many successes."

"What does this Dr. Ulrich have to do with Uncle Ivan? Why did he join you both for lunch? Are they collaborating together on a project?"

"I suggested that Ivan consult with him regarding your father's illness. After all, a second opinion is of paramount importance, particularly in your father's situation. Being an oncologist in cancer research, he may be aware of more than your Dr. Brooks, who does not specialize in oncology."

"Of course, you're absolutely right, Alan. Even though I do have total confidence in Richard Brooks, we should have a second opinion. When will he be seeing Dad?"

"Very soon. I think possibly even today. He mentioned that sometimes using a different method of administering chemotherapy may give the patient several more years of remission."

"Alan, that sounds very promising. Why didn't you tell me this yesterday?"

"I didn't want to get your hopes up until after Dan examined your father and had something positive to say. That's understandable, isn't it?"

"Yes, Alan, it is, and I'm very sorry for mistrusting you. I hope you'll forgive my dreadful behavior."

"Only if you promise never to do it again. Hey, I'm going to be late for work if I don't get moving."

Alan gave his wife a quick peck on the nose, grabbed his briefcase from a nearby chair, and hurried out the door. Melanie quickly dialed the phone in an attempt to reach Greg before he left for his office.

Greg was straightening his tie as the phone rang. "Hello," he said. "Yes, Melanie, what is it?"

"I spoke with Alan, and he told me that Dr. Ulrich from the New England Cancer Research Institute consulted with Uncle Ivan about seeing Dad. He's been doing some research on chemotherapy drugs and would like to put Dad on his study. That's what the mystery is all about."

"A second opinion does sound logical, Melanie. Although I don't understand all of this covert behavior."

"Alan told me that he didn't want me to know until Dr. Ulrich had something positive to say about Dad.

"Who is this Dr. Ulrich, and where did he come from?" Greg was not satisfied with the information. There were too many holes in the story.

"He's someone Alan knew a long time ago as a client. Apparently, he's been in touch with Alan again." She then related the incident about the young girl and the malpractice suit.

"That was really very unfortunate for him. Richard Brooks will have to decide whether Dr. Ulrich's study is worth a try. When is he going to see Dad?"

"Alan told me that it might be today."

"Good, the sooner he sees him, the better I will feel. What I don't understand is why Ivan was being so evasive. Why would he keep this from me? I'm not thoroughly convinced, Melanie, that you know the whole story."

Chapter 8

Later that morning, Dr. Dan Ulrich was with Mac, examining him and going over all of his previous test results.

He spoke at length with Dr. Brooks about the treatment that was presently being given. "I've been working on a research project of my own," he said with some deliberation. "It's been my pet project for several years now, and it is proving to be quite successful. The majority of patients who have been entered in on the study are leukemia patients. Some have Hodgkin's disease, and others have lymphosarcoma. Many of them have gone into remission and have not had a setback. I'm really proud of this breakthrough. Occasionally, you will find a patient who does not respond to treatment, but then, you will find that true in any branch of medicine."

Dr. Brooks was very confident that this was the man who would turn things around for Mac and reverse his disease. "Mac was going into remission and we were planning to discharge him soon. However, his condition suddenly seemed to deteriorate again, and today, he seems somewhat weakened. If he continues on this downhill course, I think we should consider him a candidate for your study. What do you say, Dr. Ulrich?"

"Yes, I would be willing to do this, but we must have his permission, of course. This is still experimental, and as I said before, some patients, although a very small percentage, do not respond."

Dr. Brooks extended his hand to Dr. Ulrich, and they both firmly shook in mutual agreement. "Thank you for the consultation, Dr. Ulrich. I'll be in touch."

Dr. Brooks went into Mac's room, hoping to find him in good spirits. Instead, Mac was sitting very still, staring out of the window, engrossed in something that seemed of great importance. "Hi, Mac, what's happening out there that has absorbed all of your attention?"

Mac turned toward the door, hardly changing his stern expression. "There's life going on out there. There's death taking over in here."

Dr. Brooks was rather taken aback by his unexpected reply. "Mac, I can't believe you said that! Death takes over only where it is welcomed. So far, you have done a tremendous job fighting this disease. Don't give up now that we've been thinking of sending you home. We need this bed for someone who is really ill."

Mac turned back to the window. "My time has come, Richard. I believe that when your time is up, there's nothing that anyone can do to prevent it from happening."

"Well, I'm an optimist, Mac, and I don't believe that's true. If you want something badly enough, you will ultimately get it. But you have to be persistent and believe in yourself. Don't you want to go home, Mac?"

"Of course I do. Do you think I enjoy lying around here, being poked and prodded? I'd like to leave right now, if I could. Just say the word, Doc, and I'll get dressed and call a cab."

"If you show me some improvement, the kind you exhibited a few days ago, you'll be out of this hospital very shortly. That's a promise, Mac. Nothing gives me more pleasure and satisfaction than discharging one of my patients. To me, it means a job well done, a great accomplishment."

"And what if one of your patients dies? How does that make you feel?"

Dr. Brooks hesitated a moment, knowing full well what Mac was getting at, that he was referring to himself. "Well, Mac, I wish that I could save them all. Unfortunately, that isn't possible, but I do everything I can for all of my patients. Some are stronger and more persistent fighters than others. Those with a strong will to live generally seem to have a better chance of survival. Studies have shown that being in a positive frame of mind, in many cases, is a great help in recovery. Do you understand my point, Mac?"

"Yes, Richard, I know exactly what you're saying, but not all people deserve a second chance at life. After all, life is a precious commodity and should be cherished and respected. Otherwise, it becomes fleeting and elusive and is quickly lost."

As Dr. Brooks stared at Mac with curiosity inscribed over his face, he suddenly felt someone take his arm. He turned to see Lenore standing next to him, looking fresh and rested and smiling warmly.

"What is all this chatter about, you two?" Lenore asked. "Both of you look much too sullen for such a lovely day."

"Lenore Stone, what a lovely sight you are. When you're around, the sun is always shining." Dr. Brooks then took her arm and linked it with his. "What a lucky man you are, Mac, to have such a wonderful wife who cheerfully visits you every day."

Mac broke into a broad grin for the first time in several hours. "Yes, I am very lucky to have such a wonderful wife and also a terrific family. They've put up with me for a long time. I couldn't ask for more."

"But you've had that and more today," interrupted Dr. Brooks. "What about that special visitor you had, Dr. Dan Ulrich." He then looked at Lenore. "Mac had a workup done by a research doctor from the cancer institute today. He's doing a study on patients who have the same problem as your husband. He claims to have had much success and would like to enter Mac on his study."

Lenore squeezed the doctor's arm, feeling very pleased. "That sounds very hopeful, Richard. Is it some kind of miracle drug that he has discovered?"

"Not exactly, but it's a controversial drug. He is using it in conjunction with another, and this combination seems to be doing wonders. This, of course, is experimental and can be toxic in some cases. Therefore, the patient is put on his study only if he does not respond to any other treatment.

With Mac, we have found this to be true just recently. We'll have Dr. Ulrich's findings on Mac's status later today."

"Well, I'll be very eager to know what he has to say. You will let me know as soon as you hear from Dr. Ulrich, won't you, Richard?"

"Of course, I will, Lenore."

"I don't want any more medication," Mac exclaimed. I refuse to take anything that will make me feel sick. I have had enough of this experimentation!"

"Mac, be reasonable," Dr. Brooks replied. "It's worth the trouble if it saves your life. You have only one other choice, and that's a bone marrow transplant. I would recommend going on the study instead. Mac's last bone marrow aspiration showed an increase in lymphocytes. It's important that we do one or the other. You think about it, Mac."

As Dr. Brooks turned to leave, a hospital volunteer stopped to read the number of Mac's room. She then proceeded into the room, carrying an envelope in her hand. "Mr. Stone, we have some mail for you today." She handed the envelope to Mac and turned to observe the numerous cards displayed in the room. "You certainly have a large collection of cards. Isn't it nice to know that people are thinking of you?" Without waiting for an answer, she went on. "Well, have a good day." She quickly waddled out in her crisp pink smock and her practical shoes, making a brisk clatter on the floor as she left.

Mac opened the envelope as Lenore curiously watched him. He pulled out something that appeared to be a note and read it several times. He then put it back into the envelope without saying a word.

"What is it, Mac dear?" Lenore asked, looking very puzzled. "Is it something from the lab? Won't you let me read it?"

Feeling rather troubled, Mac held on rigidly to the mysterious envelope, wondering what to do next. After some deliberation, which seemed like an eternity, Mac finally spoke. "It's something I prefer not to bother you with, Lenore."

"But, Mac," she replied, not able to contain herself, "you must tell me what it is. There's something terribly wrong, isn't there? I can read it all over your face. Please, dear, share this with me." She looked at him with pleading eyes.

"It's really nothing terribly unusual. I've received similar notes in the past." Mac was hedging to give himself time to think. He didn't want to worry Lenore. She had enough on her mind already. But he had to tell her something. "Someone is simply trying to frighten me. It's really silly—a meaningless threat. Believe me. There's nothing to worry about."

Lenore refused to be put off like this. "A threat? What kind of threat? Mac, how do you know for sure that it's nothing to worry about? Now please, dear, let me read it. You simply must!" She was almost frantic with worry to think that someone would be threatening a man who is not well and is in the hospital! How cruel to do such a thing to one who is so vulnerable, she thought, sitting at the edge of her chair, clutching nervously to the bed rail.

"Calm down, love. Believe me, it's nothing," Mac replied as he thought back to the note, which Ivan had also recently received. Not only were they harassing Ivan and Mac but they were now also threatening another member of the family. This he could not bear. The situation in which he found himself was difficult enough without the anxiety of possibly his family becoming involved. He would do anything. Keeping his family safe was of utmost importance to him.

Lenore continued to plead with her husband, trying to coerce him into showing her the note that he had received. She then remembered another incident that seemed rather strange and could very possibly be related. With quivering nerves, she attempted to give an account of her conversation with her daughter-in-law. "Just recently, Vanessa mentioned to me that Marissa thought she was being followed by a tall man wearing sunglasses and a baseball cap. She noticed him as she returned home from an errand. He was sitting in a car parked a short distance from their home. Then, another time, while she was in the library, looking for a few good books to read during the summer, she saw him walk into the library. He took out a book at random and sat down in one of the chairs available for reading. Occasionally, she would look in his direction, and each time, he seemed to be observing her. As she was leaving, Marissa stopped to get a drink from a water fountain near the entrance and saw the man walk out."

Mac appeared a bit agitated about this new information. His emotions were becoming more difficult to conceal. He suspected that there might be a connection between this man and the notes that he was receiving. "When did Marissa first notice that this man was following her or appearing everywhere that she went?"

Lenore thought for a moment. "Well, it seems to me that Vanessa said it was a few weeks ago. Marissa noticed him as she left a gift shop not far from here and was about to cross the street to where her car had been parked. There he was sitting in his car. He called to her and asked if she could give him directions to a particular restaurant. From that point on, she had observed him watching her. Vanessa and Greg felt that she was simply imagining the fact that he was following her. But now, in light of the fact that you're being threatened, I'm beginning to wonder. Do you suppose there is a connection, Mac?"

"I certainly hope not, but if this continues or if he approaches her again, we may have to do something about it. Have Greg and Vanessa seen this man?"

"No, Marissa is the only one who's been seeing him. We must find out more about him and, more precisely, what he looks like. I suppose it could all be a coincidence, or he might even be an admirer. After all, Marissa is such an attractive young girl. She always seems to have an abundance of male attention, much to her father's dismay. She's been seeing an awful lot of that young intern, Paul Glasser, lately. He seems to be a very nice young man. In fact, Greg and Vanessa are very approving of him and of his good taste in young women, I might add."

* * *

Later in the day, when Lenore left to get something to eat, Mac summoned Alan to give him the remainder of the letter. Everything he had wished to be revealed after his demise, but not before, would be sealed in an envelope.

Alan had brought the first portion of the letter that Mac had written previously. He opened his briefcase and pulled out the envelope.

"I want to combine the remaining segment of the letter with the first one," Mac said as he sealed the letter, along with some small pieces of paper, into the large envelope. "It's important that this be kept confidential, Alan. Place it back again under lock and key with my will. Make sure that it is given to Greg to be read after you have read the will."

"Don't worry, Mac," Alan said. "I'll be sure to follow your instructions precisely."

"Then that will be all for today. Thank you so much, Alan. Give my love to Melanie and the boys."

"I certainly will, Mac. Why don't you get some rest now. You seem very tired. Melanie will be on my back again if she finds out that I was here for business purposes."

"She won't find out if you don't tell her, Alan. Now, if you don't mind, I think I will take that nap." Mac turned away from Alan and pulled the covers over his shoulder.

About one hour later, after Lenore returned, Marissa appeared in the doorway of Mac's room, looking very chic in her beige silk dress, which was a lovely contrast to her long, dark hair. She wore a couple of delicate, shimmering gold chains around her neck and beige leather shoes to match her dress. She walked in and greeted her grandparents with a kiss and a little hug. Mac had just awakened from his nap and was very pleased to see her. He looked her over very carefully with a sense of pride. "Where are you going all dressed up in your Ives Saint Laurent original?" he teased.

"Paul and I are going to dinner and the theater tonight," Marissa responded with a slight giggle. Paul knows that I've wanted to see this play ever since I had read all the rave reviews it's been getting." Marissa's luminescent blue eyes danced as she spoke of her latest paramour.

"You have been seeing a lot of this young man, your grandmother tells me. He must be very special to put such a gleam in your eyes, Marissa. Do you know what his intentions are?"

"He is very special to me, Grandpa, and as far as his intentions go, the only thing I know for certain is that he intends to get some training at the cancer research institute very soon. He is very excited about it and will probably devote his career to cancer research."

Lenore smiled very approvingly at her granddaughter. "That's very commendable, dear. I certainly hope that he gets his wish. He seems to know what he wants out of life. Both your father and grandfather have always possessed that same quality of decisiveness."

"You know, Grandmother, he does remind me of both of them in some ways. I guess that's why I'm so fond of him."

"And what's this we've been hearing about another admirer who's been following you around town?" prodded Lenore.

"I have a feeling, Grandmother, that he's not exactly an admirer. For one thing, he's a bit old for me. He's probably in his late forties. This man has been popping up everywhere and has been giving me the creeps. He always wears his proverbial sunglasses, which prevent anyone from seeing his eyes."

"Do you think that you could describe him a little better for us, honey?" Mac requested, hoping to obtain more pertinent information.

Marissa began to pace back and forth retrospectively with feelings of anxiety filtering through. "He has dark brown hair, well-streaked with gray, from what I can see, and wears a baseball cap. He's tall, average weight, but a little paunchy around the middle. I can't think of anything else that was particularly unusual about him." Tiny furrows appeared between Marissa's brows as she attempted to jar her memory of the man's face. Suddenly, her face brightened a little. "I remember something else," she said. "He has a small chip on his front tooth. I wondered why he had never had it repaired."

"Those are excellent observations, Marissa, especially the chipped tooth," Mac replied, hoping that this bit of evidence would be very helpful in finding this man's identity, should the need arise.

Mac loved all three of his grandchildren, but Marissa was always very special to him. He looked forward to her visits and enjoyed teasing her from time to time. Marissa, in turn, was very devoted and attentive to him and her grandmother. They had always enjoyed a good relationship from the time Marissa was a baby. So it was only natural that they felt very protective of her and could not bear to see any harm come to her.

"Well, I have to run," exclaimed Marissa as she glanced at her watch. "It's getting late, and I must track down my date to see if he's ready to take me out." She leaned over the bed and kissed Mac goodbye. "Take care of yourself, Grandpa."

"You too, Marissa," Mac replied. "And have a good time. Let me know if you happen to see that mystery man again."

Marissa waved to her grandparents and left the hospital room.

* * *

Marissa and Paul walked hand in hand out into the lobby of the theater amid a crowd of people.

"I love the music from Camelot," Marissa exclaimed. "I've loved it ever since we did the play in high school. It wasn't as spectacular, of course, as this production."

"Did you have a part in it?" Paul asked as he turned toward Marissa.

"No, but I was in charge of getting the programs printed, selling tickets, and getting patrons. I had a staff of seven people who helped with the arrangements. It was all very exciting, even though it was a lot of work."

"I can imagine," Paul mused. "But somehow, I picture you as Lady Guinevere, the romantic leading lady. Of course, I'd be very jealous of the guy who played Lancelot."

"You didn't even know me then, silly," Marissa said with amusement.

"It doesn't matter. You'll find that I'm very possessive when you're concerned, Marissa."

"Well, you don't have to worry, Paul. I'm not seeing anyone else but you."

They reached the theater parking lot and walked over to where Paul's car had been parked. He unlocked the door on the passenger side and opened the door for Marissa with a gallant gesture.

As Paul slipped down into his sports car, he noticed that Marissa appeared rather distraught. "Paul, my ruby ring is missing." She stared unbelievingly at her right hand, trying to remember what had happened.

The ring had Marissa's birthstone mounted in a delicate gold setting. She had received it from her grandmother on her eighteenth birthday, a year ago. It belonged to Marissa's great-grandmother, who shared the same birthstone, a brilliant ruby.

"The last time I remember seeing it was in the restaurant after dinner."

"Yes, I remember seeing it too," Paul said. "You took it off so that I could get a better look at it, and then you left for the powder room."

"When I got back to the table, I had completely forgotten about it. Paul, what did you do with the ring?"

"I put it in a small saucer so that it would not be accidentally knocked to the floor by a waiter clearing our table. By the time you returned to the table, I completely forgot about the ring too. I'm really sorry, Marissa."

"I must get that ring back. It meant so much to me."

"We'll go back to the restaurant and inquire about it. Don't worry, Marissa. We'll find it."

They drove back to the restaurant, which was located a couple of blocks away from the theater.

Paul spoke to the maître d', giving him an account of what had happened, and asked if the ring had been found.

The maître d' left for a few minutes while he checked with the waiters to see if anyone of them had found the ring. He also had one of them check the table and the floor underneath, but it was to no avail. The ring was gone.

"Someone must have realized its worth and had stolen it," Paul said as he tried to comfort Marissa by putting his arm around her.

Marissa had tears in her eyes as they left the restaurant without the ruby ring.

Chapter 9

With the expansion of Stone Pharmaceutical Labs, Greg was kept very busy, occasionally working till very late. He presently devised a plan to set up offices and a factory in France; after which, he intended to eventually expand to England, Italy, or Australia. Greg took occasional trips to find the property he wished to acquire for the site. He also planned to rent a temporary facility until a factory could be constructed according to his specifications.

On one occasion, he took with him his brother-in-law, Alan, the legal adviser for the firm. However, he seemed extremely reluctant to make the trip at this time. Greg was puzzled by his reticence to leave home but was finally able to convince him to go. Today, Greg had his secretary make arrangements for him to make another trip. It was going to be Paris, and this time, David Warner, the temporary chairman of the board, was to accompany him.

Greg's secretary buzzed him to let him know that his reservations for the trip were made and also that Renée Bordeaux was waiting in the outer office to speak to him.

"Did she say what she wanted? Never mind, send her in." Greg hoped that she wasn't coming to him with some involved problem that would consume too much of his time. He didn't need any distractions while he prepared all the details for his trip.

Renée walked into Greg's office with her usual confident air. She closed the door and sat down in the chair across from Greg. She crossed her legs high, revealing a portion of her well-shaped thigh from a slit in her skirt. She wore very high heels, which accentuated her slender legs.

Greg inadvertently admired her appearance. He found her to be attractive to the point of distraction. However, he did not wish to reveal this to her now.

Renée studied his mood for a moment. She hoped that he would be receptive to the suggestion she was about to make. "I hear that you are planning another trip to France in a couple of days. Is that correct?"

"Yes, that is correct, Renée," he replied, "with Dave Warner, our new temporary board chairman."

Renée then continued. "Would it be possible for me to take this trip with you?" Without giving him the opportunity to refuse, she continued to speak very quickly. "It would give me the opportunity to visit my family whom I have not seen in quite some time. I could also learn something about this new expansion that you've been working on. Please don't refuse me, Greg. I would appreciate it immensely." She observed his reaction to her request but was certain what his reply would be.

"All the arrangements have been made, Renée. We have a very busy schedule planned with much work to do." Greg's stern face began to soften as he reflected a moment. He then looked into her eyes, which were now pleading with him. "However," he continued, "I don't think it would be too much trouble to make a reservation for you too. We'll be leaving the day after tomorrow. Can you be ready by then?"

Renée was almost rendered speechless as she heard Greg's reply to her plea. However, she quickly regained her composure, as well as her voice. "Why, of course, I can be ready. You can be sure of that. Thank you for being so considerate." Renée was amazed at how easily she was able to cajole him into letting her go along to Paris with them even though it was apparent at first that he did not think it was such a good idea. This knowledge excited her so that it brought a flush to her cheeks. "I will leave now and make preparations for the trip. *Merci beaucoup!*" She smiled ecstatically and then left for her office.

Greg buzzed his secretary and then gave her instructions to make reservations for Ms. Bordeaux as well.

He then called David Warner to discuss some last-minute business matters. Greg also mentioned the fact that Renée Bordeaux was to accompany them to Paris. "I feel that she will be quite an asset to us on this trip," he said. "People are just naturally drawn to her, and they seem to want to please her. I've even found myself doing that from time to time. She is a good salesperson and speaks French. I feel she's almost a necessity."

"That's fine with me, Greg," David remarked. "Not only is she good but she's charming and humorous as well. With her along, the trip should be very enjoyable."

Greg agreed but quickly reminded him that there was a lot of work to be done once they arrived in France, and there wouldn't be much time for frivolity.

Chapter 10

That evening, Greg and his wife, Vanessa, decided to pay Mac a visit. While en route to the hospital, there was much tension apparent between them.

"Why is it so imperative that you take this trip to France now?" Vanessa asked rather tersely. "I'm so worried about Marissa's safety. What if that man who seems to be following her is not a coincidence? She may be in real danger, Greg."

"I can't drop everything and accompany Marissa everywhere she goes. Be realistic, Van. There are a lot of important business transactions that must be attended to in France right now, and the trip cannot be postponed." Feelings of anger began to surface. Greg did not want anything or anyone to interfere with his vital business venture.

However, it was difficult for Vanessa to understand why this trip took precedence over everything, including his family. "Don't you care about us? Aren't you the least bit concerned about your daughter's safety?"

"Look, Van, I care, but my being here won't change anything. Don't you see that? If you feel threatened at any time while I am away, simply call the police."

Vanessa could not believe her husband's insensitivity and remained silent until they reached the hospital.

On the elevator, Greg turned toward his wife and observed her depressed state. "Come on, Van. When we get home, I'll show you how much I do care." He put his arm around her. He then lowered it so that his hand came to rest on her buttocks, and he gave her a gentle tap.

As the elevator doors opened, Vanessa pulled away from Greg and walked out. He then followed her out quickly. "What's wrong, Van?"

She looked at him with disdain. "What I need is your emotional support. If you can't give me that, then don't expect me to be there for you physically. Is that all you think I need to make everything all right?"

Greg looked away from her and did not answer. This was not the time or the place to have an argument. Besides, nothing she could say would dissuade him from putting forth his plans. His determination was established.

As they reached his room, Mac was sitting in a chair, and Lenore was sitting next to him. They were holding hands and conversing quietly. Greg and Vanessa walked in and greeted them warmly.

"It's good to see you two again," Mac announced. "You don't very often grace us with your company."

"I know, Dad," Greg replied. "I've been very busy lately. You know how it is." He had avoided visiting with his father because he could not face him with the news that he was going against his father's wishes and enlarging the company further. Mac might not have been able to handle the trauma it would create.

But Greg could not hold it back any longer. His father had to be told no matter what the consequences might be. Now that the wheels were in motion, there was no turning back. For the first time, he had made a decision of such magnitude involving the company without first consulting with his father. Greg needed a sense of independence. After all, he was a grown man with visions and aspirations of his own.

"Well, you certainly are looking good this evening," Vanessa said to Mac. "Almost well enough to go home."

Lenore smiled at her daughter-in-law and then admirably surveyed her husband. "Everyone around here keeps telling Mac that if he stabilized and remains that way, he'll be discharged soon."

"That's terrific, Dad," Greg replied. "I knew you were a man made of steel."

"Correction," Mac interrupted, "a man made of stone."

Greg acknowledged his father's pun with amusement. "Is it possible that by the time I get home from my trip, you'll be at the office waiting for me?"

"Well, Greg, that's entirely possible. Where, may I ask, are you going on this trip?"

"I'm going to France, Dad, to make plans for an expansion there."

It was finally out in the open. He explained his motives and why it was an important move for the company. He also described what had already transpired and what more had to be done for the completion of the project.

"Eventually," Greg continued, "I intend to broaden our base even further, to tap England, Australia, or Italy."

A hint of disbelief appeared in Mac's eyes as he listened to what his son was revealing to him. He had not been consulted about this. Yet he could not help but feel intrigued by these overwhelming plans that Greg was going to make a reality.

"This comes as somewhat of a surprise, son. Although you seem to have given your project plenty of thought, I would like to hear more about it."

Lenore also listened intently to her son relate the entire scenario and became very excited about these new prospects. She recognized her son's ambition and his tremendous drive for power as very similar to what his father had expressed when he was Greg's age. *Greg certainly is his father's son,* she thought.

The conversation continued at length. Mac wanted to warn his son that he should be careful not to become overzealous with his ambition but resolved not to interfere. At that moment, he decided that it was finally time to let go. It was a natural progression of life. He had to step aside. His own ailment had made that decision for him. "All of your plans appear to be very sound. I wish you much luck."

Greg shook his father's hand and then kissed him on his cheek. "Thank you, Dad, for understanding."

Lenore stood up and kissed her son. "I wish you a good and very successful trip." She then turned to Vanessa and asked, "Are you going with him, Vanessa? It would be a good opportunity for you to see Paris."

Recalling the argument that she had with Greg on their way to the hospital concerning Marissa's safety and some of the problems that their relationship was experiencing lately, Vanessa had not even considered going this time. "There will be so much business to contend with in Paris." Vanessa felt rather disturbed but did not wish to express her feelings to her mother-in-law. "Maybe I'll take the trip another time. Greg has too much work to do and might not have time for sightseeing. He'll be going back again very soon, I'm sure, so there'll be many more opportunities for me to go later."

"Of course," Lenore replied. "You know what's best for you, dear. If you should get lonely while Greg is away, you can visit with us. It's always good to see you."

Greg and Vanessa left for home and remained in almost complete silence until they arrived at their doorstep. Vanessa opened the door, and as she walked into the house with Greg a couple of steps behind her, she reflected upon the conversation back at the hospital about the trip and felt a need for reassurance. "I will go to France with you the next time, won't I, Greg? Hopefully, by then, we will be assured of Marissa's safety."

"Yes, Van, of course you will," he replied. "The next time, there won't be as much work to do. I'll make certain of that. We can shop, do some sightseeing, and whatever else you would like to do, I promise. Maybe Marissa could go along too."

Vanessa was pleased that her husband expressed concern for her, but she could not help wondering if he would keep his word. For Greg, Stone Pharmaceuticals always took precedence over everything. Nothing was held sacred when a business matter beckoned. The pharmaceutical company was an overwhelming competitor and a voracious time consumer. Vanessa found it to be a most difficult contender. However, she was not one who complained a great deal. She was able to control her emotions well, on most occasions.

Chapter 11

The gleaming silvery jet flashed through the vivid blue sky like a streak of lightning breaking through an occasional vaporous cloud formation. Renée sat by the window, admiring nature's artistic beauty unfolding before her. She could only vaguely hear the conversation between Greg and David Warner. They seemed to be referring to a schedule they planned to follow once the plane landed in Paris.

Renée looked forward to this trip and the opportunity it was giving her to visit her family and some of the friends she had left behind when she came to America to pursue her career.

Her marriage had ended, a culmination of insurmountable problems; after which, Renée had thrown herself into her work until it became an obsession. In Paris, she worked in sales for an advertising agency. At the beginning, it was very difficult; however, eventually she established a good repertoire of clientele, making success inevitable. When she came to America, she had gained enough experience to acquire a position at Stone Pharmaceutical Labs.

Renée rarely thought about her dreadful marriage experience until now. She had received a letter from her parents a month ago telling of her former husband's marriage to a wealthy business woman. Jean Claude Bordeaux was an artist who scarcely earned enough money to support himself. He possessed talent but had little drive and ambition to become successful. He, therefore, chose a woman ten years his senior who could support him in a style that he enjoyed. It was a marriage of convenience rather than one of love and burning passion.

With Renée, there had been love and passion until their relationship had begun straining at the seams. Jean rarely worked, and Renée had been in the process of trying to establish a career. Consequently, Jean had such an abundance of time that he thought nothing of entertaining himself with the company of other women. He never even spared Renée by making an attempt to be discreet. For him, they were mere playthings, but Renée found his behavior an affront to their marriage. She confronted him with the serious effect that his actions were having on their relationship. However, her pleas merely elicited an apathetic response that repudiated any lingering belief that their marriage could have been saved.

After their divorce, Renée decided to get as far away from the painful reminders of the past as possible. She decided to leave France. However, as a result, she missed her parents and her friends. This trip was her first opportunity to visit with them again, and she immensely looked forward to it.

When they arrived in Paris, Greg and David continued with their organizing and planning and spent much of the time making phone calls and appointments. Renée went on to Chantilly to visit her family.

Chantilly was a pleasant resort town twenty-five miles north of Paris. For Renée, it was easily accessible by car. She had rented a small Peugeot for the day and drove to her parents' home. It was a modest white frame house nestled in a grove of stately green trees. What a joy to behold, Renée thought, as she pulled up to the front of the house. To her, the house was a representation of her childhood and all the memories that revolved around it.

It was a wonderful reunion for them all. Not only did she see her parents but also her aunts, uncles, cousins, and friends gathered for a joyous party, welcoming Renée back home even though it was for such a short time. She promised that, after this, there would certainly be more return trips in the near future. Her parents expressed great pride in the overwhelming success Renée was having and longed to hear all about her life in America and about all her accomplishments.

Her parents made every attempt to make Renée's visit a memorable occasion. She was ecstatically happy renewing old experiences with everyone.

Finally, there had to be one incident that would mar the enchantment of the reunion. After most of the people had left the party, the doorbell rang unexpectedly. When Renée opened the door, she was startled by the appearance of Jean Claude Bordeaux, her former husband. She stared at him apprehensively, wondering why he had come to see her.

"Renée, it's wonderful to see you again," he said in French. "I heard from your friend Nicole that you were coming back home for a visit. I simply had to see you again. Please forgive me." He took her left hand in his right and held it for a moment. He then looked down at it and made an observation. "You are not wearing any rings. I'm relieved to see that no suitor has claimed you."

"What difference would that make to you, Jean? I heard that you were married," she said.

"Yes, I married Monique Marche. She is a very pleasant woman and is very good to me."

"I'm glad to hear that you're happy and that you've finally settled down."

"Oh, my dear Renée, I may be reasonably happy, but one could never say that I've settled down. For me that is not possible. Life would become much too dull."

"Yes, as I recall, you always did require change." She then motioned to the doorway. "Would you like to come in?"

"No, I was not invited to your party, but I would like to speak with you. Can we go somewhere? Most of your friends and family have gone."

"I don't think that I care to go anywhere with you, Jean."

"Oh come on, Renée. A little conversation won't hurt you."

"Well, If you insist," she said with some reluctance. "Come on then, let's take a walk." Renée closed the door to the house and followed Jean toward the road. "I hear that you have married well. Your wife is some kind of business woman."

"Yes, Monique has a chain of boutiques in Paris and London. In fact, she left this morning for London to check on a few of them."

"You never accompany her on her trips?"

"Yes, I've gone on several trips with her, but this time I made excuses so that I could see you."

"Am I supposed to be flattered, Jean?"

"You can be whatever you want. But I simply needed to see you again. You were my wife, and you will always mean a great deal to me. I've never stopped loving you, Renée. The divorce was your idea, if you recall. I never found good reason for it. However, women get emotional over things of little importance. So you wanted our marriage to end. But now that you are able to assess our relationship objectively, what do you think? Could we still be friends, Renée?"

"I don't know, Jean. The hurt is over with and gone, of course. It's been a long time, and time heals all wounds. But I don't think I can feel anything at all for you anymore, not friendship, not love, not even hostility. I've blotted your memory out of my mind completely, never expecting to see you again. When I heard that you were married, I was very pleased."

"Why were you pleased, that I could no longer be a threat to you?" He paused, stopped walking, and took hold of her. "If you allowed yourself to feel anything for me, what would that be? Are you afraid that it might be passion?" He looked squarely into her eyes.

She hesitated for a moment and then spoke. "That may have been all I ever did feel for you. We consumed each other with passion. The fire was meant to burn out. A relationship needs more than that. What about respect, trust, and admiration? Our relationship never had any of those qualities. It was never meant to last."

"You are living a fantasy, Renée. You expect too much. No one can live up to your expectations."

"Don't be too sure of that. Not all men were made out of the same mold. Someday, I will have a man who possesses all the qualities which I find to be admirable. You just wait and see."

They had walked till they were feeling tired and then returned to the house.

"Can I see you again before you leave?" he asked as they reached the front door. "I would love to show you some of my work. Your opinion is important to me."

"No, Jean, I don't think so. There won't be any more time left. I am here to work you know. But it is good to hear that you are painting again."

"Yes, I've been preparing for an exhibit soon. Nothing would please me more than to have you there. Will you be back soon again?"

"I don't know when I will be back. It all depends upon how much is accomplished during this trip."

"Well, then come with me now to my house. You can see my studio where I work and all of my paintings displayed there."

"No, I can't this time. I'm very tired, Jean, and I must say good-bye."

"This is very disappointing to me, Renée. However, I'll accept your decision, if you promise to let me know the next time you are in France."

"Oh—perhaps."

"Well then, good-bye for now, Renée." He leaned toward her and attempted to kiss her on the mouth. But she quickly averted him, and he kissed her on the cheek.

"Have it your way, Renée," he said and turned to leave.

Chapter 12

The following day, Renée accompanied Greg and David to all the business meetings, assisting with translation, being introduced to many people, and absorbing more knowledge in the process of expansion.

Four days went by with much intense work, and on the fourth evening, they decided to celebrate their successful and very fruitful trip.

A dinner party was being held in the Hotel Plaza Athénée, where they stayed, coinciding with their plans for a celebration. There was a band for entertainment and dancing to add to the festivities.

Greg and David left their respective rooms and reached the dining room at approximately the same time. They both wore dark suits, white shirts and dark ties, giving them a crisp, fresh, and formal appearance. Greg was the taller and younger one of the two distinguished gentlemen.

They were led to a table by the maître d', who sat them down in a cozy nook to one side of the dining room.

"Hope we don't have to wait too long for the beautiful member of our party," David remarked. "I'm starved."

Greg looked around to see if Renée was on her way into the dining room. "So am I, but it seems women fuss so much when they're celebrating a special occasion. It invariably takes them longer to get ready."

"Yes," David acknowledged, "my wife is always the last one in the family to be ready when we're going out. Of course, having had two boys, she's the only woman in the house."

Their waiter came by, and they ordered drinks. When he left with the order, Greg turned to the entrance of the large room once more, searching for Renée. "There she is now, looking lovelier than ever."

"Yes," David agreed as he turned to see Renée walking toward them with a certain elegance that was singular. "Now that was well worth waiting for." He said this with a small chortle.

She walked toward them in a beautifully flowing white silk dress that revealed her slender figure. Her gleaming smile wreathed her face with beauty as she approached the two men at the table. "Have you been waiting very long, gentlemen," she asked, looking at each one of them.

David was the first to answer. "It seemed like hours, but it doesn't matter anymore. You've joined us, and you look absolutely stunning."

Renée lowered her eyes for a moment and then looked back at him. "Thank you, David. How kind of you to say so."

In a few moments, the waiter returned and took their dinner orders. The dining room was beginning to fill up with people attired in elegant evening clothes, creating a festive mood throughout. There was candlelight at each table, giving a luminous quality and serene appearance to the enormous room. The waiters, dressed in black, were seen ambulating about with large silver trays being balanced at the shoulder, bearing sparkling vintage champagne or deliciously aromatic, piping hot gourmet dishes.

Greg, David, and Renée discussed their grand business triumphs over their drinks.

"We've accomplished a lot this trip." Greg glowed with delight.

"Yes," David replied, "just acquiring the two buildings for our facility was quite a find. There's very little that needs to be done with them. We were very lucky."

"It previously had been a small bottling factory," Renée stated. "And the building adjacent to it had been a lab. That was perfect."

"Yes, we were very lucky," Greg acknowledged. "But we still need to search for land to build our own facility. It's not a good idea to lease. But of course, it will have to do for now. It is a vehicle we're going to use for the commencement of our expansion." Greg's exhilaration was vividly apparent. This event was to mark a turning point in his life. He had planned for this for quite some time, and he was now going to witness the reality of his dream.

Then, with great efficiency and a flourish, the waiter presented to them their dinners. He then walked very sprightly away, as a gust of wind blows through the trees and suddenly vanishes.

"We have all of our business matters completed for now, "Greg remarked. "It's good to be able to relax and enjoy our dinner."

David took a drink of wine and looked up at Greg. "Why don't we stay another day for some sightseeing? Then for the evening entertainment, we could pull a few strings and get tickets to the Lido."

"Oh très jolie!" Renée exclaimed. "That would be *magnifique*! Could we do that, Greg?" Renée became caught up with the excitement of the evening and the anticipation of a holiday.

"Well, maybe we could arrange that," Greg replied sheepishly. "But I will have to call the office tomorrow morning to see if we'll be missed for another day. If we can be spared, then we will stay. That is a promise. I'll make the arrangements myself."

Renée put her hand on Greg's arm. "You are a wonderful man to work for, Greg. I am so happy that you let me take this trip with you."

After they had completed their dinners, the waiter came over to clear the table. David asked to be excused and left the table to call home.

In a little while, the band began to play a soft, orchestrated melody, and several couples emerged on the dance floor.

Renée turned to Greg, and an ingratiating smile touched her lips. "You must be an excellent dancer. You are good at so many things."

He gazed at her with enigmatic appraisal. Renée continuously amazed him. She was always able to maneuver him so easily and so remarkably well. He was now going to ask her to dance because she had purposely led him to do so. After scrutinizing her for a moment, he asked her to dance, as he knew she wished.

The music continued to play, one enchanting piece after another. They walked out onto the dance floor, and Greg took her into his arms.

As he did, he felt a tingling sensation in his fingers, and a feeling of excitement went through him. For a brief second, he felt his knees become flaccid. He hadn't felt this way since the very first time that he had danced with a girl. Greg found himself staring at her in admiration. She looked even lovelier, he thought, than ever before, if that was possible. Her hair was fixed with more sophistication than usual. One side of her long, raven hair was swept back with a white blossom and a scattering of baby's breath going across to the back. Her dress held on to one shoulder while the other was alluringly exposed, baring a softly tanned shoulder and arm, contrasting the white silk of her dress. He thought she looked exquisite, and he told her so.

She leaned closer to him as they continued to dance, and he placed his head tenderly against hers.

Renée felt warm and content. It was wonderful, she thought, to be held securely in a man's arms again and one whom she found so devastatingly attractive. Unfortunately, he was married, but for now, he belonged to her.

As the music stopped, Greg noticed that David had returned. "We should get back to the table or David will feel lost and abandoned."

Renée felt disappointment at having to let go of Greg. She enjoyed the feel of his muscular body against hers. But she promised herself that she'd have him again. They walked back to the table where David was sitting.

"By the look on your face, you must have become very lonely while we were dancing," Greg teased.

"Well, how would you feel?" David conjectured. "I told my wife that if everything goes well and we are not needed back, then I'll probably stay another day in Paris. And she was glad to hear it. Donna and the boys are having a great time eating pizza and hamburgers instead of having to fuss with meals."

Greg laughed at David's attempt to evoke sympathy. "Hey, Dave, stop looking for pity because you're not going to get it from us. Seems to me that you're the lucky one traveling in France."

"I'm sure that your wife would have loved to trade places with you," Renée interrupted. "But of course, she could not. Just think, tomorrow I may be giving both of you charming gentlemen a tour around Paris. What fun that will be. And what a lovely way to spend my thirty-third birthday."

"Tomorrow is your birthday, Renée?" asked David. "I'm surprised that you hadn't mentioned it before. Will your family want you to spend the day with them?"

Greg looked at Renée with some amusement. "I have a feeling that you have the entire day all planned out."

"You just may be right, Greg."

"It must be great to be only thirty-three years old and have such a high energy factor."

"I don't understand," Renée replied, "why Americans venerate youth with such fervor. To me, youth means inexperience, vulnerability, and, many times, a lack of direction and immaturity. I can't wait for each year to pass, and with it, the ability to cope with life more readily. It can be a very long and difficult road. There is so much to learn and so many obstacles to overcome. But don't get me wrong. I look forward to exploring the astonishment of life and growing with each experience. I would not want to remain young and childlike forever."

"Renée, you are a wonder!" Greg regarded her with his eyes beaming. "Your philosophy is much more sophisticated than your years. That was certainly not a description of you."

"No, you are right, at least not recently. I am more levelheaded now. But it did take a few years." Renée suddenly felt a tightening deep in the pit of her stomach. "While I lived here in France, my life was not always very pleasant."

"Did you have an unhappy childhood, Renée?" David probed.

"No, au contraire, my childhood was very pleasant. It was not until I married Jean Claude that I learned about the hardships life had to offer. We had very little money because Jean rarely worked. We also did not have a very good relationship. At first, of course, there was the grand passion. But later on, we had problems which caused us to drift apart. It was a painful experience but one through which I learned a great deal about life and also about myself."

"That's very sad, Renée. I'm very sorry," David said.

"Oh you needn't be. It's over with," she replied.

"When you reach my age, your view of life will change. You'll see the years disappearing too quickly. In youth, one has the good fortune of looking forward to a fruitful and challenging life ahead. Later in life, one has only contemplation of years gone by to reflect upon. And I am quickly reaching that stage of life. Let me be honest with you—I don't look forward to it," David mused thoughtfully.

"You won't be old for a long time to come, David," Greg said. "You will always be young in spirit."

"I can never recall wanting to be older than my years, not even when I was very young. Guess I've always been content at every age. I felt that each age had it compensations." David looked over at Renée and continued. "I'm much older than you, and I want to live forever."

"Yes, I can appreciate that," Renée responded. "I can understand your feelings, David. You have led a full life. You want to go on enjoying it for a long time to come." She stopped for a moment then continued. "I'm impatient, in comparison. I want it all right now. For me, it is too long a wait for this gradual awakening. I know I've had wonderful opportunities at Stone Labs, which I probably would not have had if Ihad remained here in France all of my life."

Greg looked at Renée with constant and unfailing admiration. He was an ambitious and enterprising man and recognized the same qualities in her. He instinctively knew that she would do well from the start and, therefore, he gave her those opportunities. He understood her impatience and that she was imbued with the will to succeed for he felt those same yearnings when he was her age and even after that. He still did.

"The music is being wasted," Renée said as she sprang to her feet. "We don't want to spend the entire evening in philosophical discussion, do we?"

"Certainly not," Greg replied. "Why don't you and David dance this one, and I'll just sit back and watch."

"Okay," David relented with a fixed gaze on Renée. "I'll show you some fancy footwork you've only seen in the old movies. It's called a fox-trot." They walked on out to the middle of the dance floor and began to dance. Renée was not familiar with David's style of dance but eventually caught on to his fancy maneuvering.

Greg watched from a distance, amused by David's remarkable dancing ability.

David danced with ease, leading Renée around the dance floor with precision and skill. Together, they looked like a couple out of an old Fred Astaire movie, Greg thought, as he watched their confident strides.

The evening went gloriously, Greg and David each taking turns dancing with Renée to the orchestrated music. Each performed in his own style, including Renée, who taught both of her male escorts a few steps of her own.

Chapter 13

Finally, at midnight, the band stopped playing. David was beginning to feel somewhat tired from imbibing in spirits and dancing and also due to the lateness of the hour. He lifted his glass of bourbon and drank it to the bottom. "You two will have to excuse me, but it's getting very late. I have to get some sleep or I won't be able to function at all tomorrow."

"We will be leaving shortly too, David," replied Greg. "See you in the morning after I've called the lab."

"If all goes well, don't forget about our rendezvous with Paris tomorrow," Renée called out to David as he departed.

After David left, Renée looked up at Greg. "Are you feeling sleepy too, Greg?"

"No, Renée, I'm fine, but maybe we should turn in as well. Like I said before, I'm going to call the lab tomorrow morning. If I'm needed back, we'll have to leave."

Renée selfishly wished that they would remain in Paris for another day. She was having too wonderful a time to end it so abruptly.

They walked out of the large elegant dining room and down a wide hallway to the elevators then up to the eighth floor, where their respective rooms were located.

Greg walked Renée down the long hallway and around the corner. Her room was in one of the glass towers that were situated on either side of the hotel. The rooms in these towers had enormous windows from floor to ceiling overlooking a magnificent view of Paris. In the shimmering sunlight, the towers took on a gleaming, golden façade that was breathtaking. At night, they glowed with the lights from the city.

Renée's room was elegantly appointed with shades of cream. The plush wall-to-wall carpeting felt luxuriously soft underfoot. On the bed was a billowy quilt in cream with matching drapery and pillows of crimson. The furnishings were Art Deco.

As they reached her door, Renée handed Greg her key. He unlocked the door and then opened it, revealing the room in its entire splendor. A lamp had been left lit on a large dressing table against the wall.

Renée took Greg's hand and led him inside. "Come in and see what Stone Labs is paying for. It is a very lovely room. I will not like leaving it behind." She closed the door behind him and led him to the windows with the resplendent view. "Take a look at Paris in the evening. Isn't it beautiful?"

"It's a terrific room," Greg agreed. "And so is Paris with all of its lights. I'm glad you're pleased. You deserve it." He paused for a moment, feeling enormously improper, and then continued. "I think it would be best if I left so that we can both get some rest."

"Oh not just yet. Please, Greg." Renée pleaded, still holding on to his hand. "Come sit down for a moment and enjoy the view." She maneuvered him into an overstuffed chair by the window and stood behind him.

His first impulse was to raise an objection and make a quick exit. But she began to massage his neck and his shoulders.

"This has been such a memorable evening," she said. "I don't ever want it to end."

He resigned himself to total submission.

Renée continued to massage his neck and then his temples, bringing his head to rest on her breasts. "This should help you to relax and forget about everything. Just concentrate on relaxing." She gently moved her hands in a circular motion till she could feel his tension releasing.

"Renée, that feels wonderful." Greg revealed his pleasure in her touch and the captivating effect she was having on him. He closed his eyes and reveled in this beguiling moment. "Renée, is there no end to your wondrous talents?"

"Hush, Greg, just sit back and stay relaxed," she said as she loosened his tie and removed it. She then proceeded to pull off his jacket. "This is very cumbersome. Why don't we take it off." Renée took the jacket and placed it on another chair nearby. She then unbuttoned three of his shirt buttons and began to stroke his upper chest. She continued down his chest, making swirling motions.

Greg was beginning to feel strongly aroused. He felt a surging awareness in his groin, a thoroughly intemperate and disconcerting state in which to be. He then grasped both of her hands very tenderly.

Renée came from behind the chair and placed herself smoothly into his lap. Her dancing dark eyes came to rest on the softness of his blue. She ran her fingers through the tuft of curly blond hair in the middle of his chest. Then, tilting her head slightly, she sought his mouth with hers. It was soft and yielding.

He responded in kind to her gentle kiss. Then he continued to kiss her over and over. His desire for her was unquenchable, and with a surge of passion, he lifted her into his arms and carried her to bed.

He gently removed the white flower from her hair then unzipped her dress and removed it in a slow-flowing motion, revealing her vivacious femininity. Greg quickly removed his clothing and put them aside. He looked into her eager, gleaming eyes and laid her back on the pillows. He then kissed her feverishly on the mouth and down the line of her slender neck, running his hands through her silken black tresses, then kissing her porcelain and gently curving shoulders and soft breasts. He caressed every part of her smooth, warm skin. Greg knew that he had longed for her but had always denied himself until now. Renée had invited him, and he found himself overwhelmed with searing desire for her.

Renée wildly matched his response with an unleashed passion, thrusting her body against his muscular physique, unable to control her surging emotions. Their bodies were molded together and flowed in rhythmic unison until they reached the full crescendo of intensity. Renée cried out with total ecstasy and fulfillment, grasping on to him with all of her strength and then releasing him.

Greg lay back filled with wonderment and exhaustion. She rested her head on his shoulder, and they fell quickly to sleep in each other's embrace.

At dawn, Renée awoke and began gently stroking Greg's chest, burying her face in the flaxen tuft of hair on his chest. She continued to lazily stroke his entire body until she reawakened his passion, and his unrelenting desire rose to meet hers. They tumbled together in each other's arms with joyous laughter and playful ecstasy all over the large bed. They made love with even more sensual intensity than before, clinging to one another voraciously until they became one.

Greg could see enormous pleasure in Renée's eyes and could feel her heart pounding against his chest. Bending down, he kissed her forehead very tenderly then proceeded to kiss her nose and finally rested his lips firmly on hers.

A couple of hours later, they were up and showering together, basking in the pleasure of each other's company.

Later, Greg got dressed in the clothes he had worn the night before while Renée sat in one of the stuffed chairs, wearing only a towel. She gazed provocatively in his direction.

"Aren't you getting dressed today?" Greg asked as he slipped into his shoes and picked up his jacket. "I'm going to my room now to change and to call my office. If there is nothing urgent waiting for me to get back to, we'll keep our rendezvous with Paris and celebrate your birthday."

"You are so thoughtful and generous, Greg. I love you for it. You are one of a kind. There's no one like you in this whole world." She got up from the chair and walked him to the door. She then put her arms around his neck and kissed him.

He returned her kiss and embrace. "I'll see you shortly. Be ready." He left for his room, which was located a short distance down the hall.

When Greg called Stone Pharmaceutical Labs, there was nothing of great significance awaiting him personally. He was able to delegate the work to his other executives and had complete confidence in their ability to perform the tasks without his guidance. "We're staying on one more day to take in some of the sights. We'll be back in time for the weekly conference to let you in on all of the developments here. I'm sure that everyone will be very interested."

Greg hung up the phone and then changed into more casual clothes. He then called David Warner and told him that they were able to stay on one more day.

"I think that I've had too much celebrating last night," David said. "You and Renée go on without me. Maybe I'll join you later today. Have a good time, and wish Renée a happy birthday. See you later, Greg."

Greg then called his wife, Vanessa, at home. "Hi, Van, how is everything?"

"Oh, Greg," Vanessa said in astonishment, "I never expected a call from you. Everything is just fine. I'm planning on going to visit your father today. Lenore called last evening and said that he wasn't himself yesterday, and she was worried about him."

"I'm sure that he'll be fine, Van. Tell Mother not to worry. The reason why I've called is that we've decided to stay another day in Paris. So don't plan on my return until sometime tomorrow. If you need to reach me, you have my cell phone number. I won't be spending much time at the hotel."

"All right, Greg. I hope that there won't be any reason for me to get in touch with you."

"Good-bye, Van. Take care." Greg hung up the phone and went back to get Renée. When he reached her room, she was waiting for him in a pale-blue casual skirt and blouse.

"You look absolutely radiant," Greg told her, holding her at arm's length. "Are you ready to give me a tour of Paris? We are staying another day."

"Oui assurément," she replied with excitement. "But where is David? Isn't he going to join us?"

"No, he isn't feeling well this morning. He said that he would probably join us later. Oh, and he wanted to wish you a happy birthday."

"That was sweet of him. But I'm truly sorry to hear that he is not feeling well."

After breakfast, Greg and Renée left the hotel together to embark on their sightseeing tour of Paris.

Their first stop was the Eiffel Tower, where they were able to envision the entire city with its superb architecture of earlier centuries.

"So what do you think of the view of Paris from here, Greg?" Renée asked, feeling a sense of pride for this beautiful city of which she was a part.

"It's like an enticing mistress that is waiting to seduce me with her charms," Greg answered and turned to gaze at her. "To me, you and this fabulous city will always be synonymous."

A broad smile illuminated her face, and she leaned toward him, kissing him on the cheek.

They walked along the broad, treelined Champs-Élysées and admired the magnificent Arc de Triomphe at the center of Place de l'Étoile, which contains the Tomb of the Unknown Soldier.

They strolled along the quais that parallels each side of the Seine River.

"Would you like to take a ride on the Bateaux Mouche, the sightseeing boat?" Renée asked, taking Greg's hand and leading him to one of the boats that was being boarded for a scenic tour on the Seine.

The Bateaux Mouche was an excursion boat that usually contained a small restaurant, snack bar, and even an orchestra.

Greg followed Renée onto the boat, and they settled into one of the seats as the boat commenced its journey. It passed the grand buildings that lined both banks of the river. They passed the Palais du Louvre, the world's largest palace and one of the most famous art museums.

They listened to the tour guide. "Here one can find such priceless works as Leonardo da Vinci's Mona Lisa. Adorning the galleries are also paintings by Cézanne, Degas, Monet, Renoir, and Van Gogh. The sculpture department contains two world-famous works: Winged Victory of Samothrace and the armless *Venus de Milo*, which Nöel Coward once described as a warning against biting your fingernails."

Greg and Renée turned to each, other sharing in the amusement. Then Greg put his arm warmly and caressingly around Renée's shoulders.

The guide continued to speak. "We now come to the cathedral of Notre-Dame in all of its Gothic glory and the small Sainte-Chapelle of King Louis IX, who reigned during the Crusades. Its stained glass lights up like a jewel in the morning sunlight."

They cruised as far as the Bois de Boulogne on the Seine, the cruise lasting for approximately two hours.

Later, they toured Montmartre, the Bohemian sector, on foot. There, one of the artists sketched a caricature of Greg and Renée together. They laughed and talked and felt the warmth and joy of each other's company.

"I have always felt much fondness for Paris, but never have I felt so much love for it as I do today," Renée confessed. "I am seeing it in a very different light through the reflection in your eyes, Greg. It has taken on a different quality, far richer than I have ever observed before."

"This is a wonderful day," Greg said, taking her hand in his. "I hope that you're enjoying your birthday."

"Oh, Greg, I cannot remember one which I have enjoyed more."

They sat down at one of the outdoor cafés to have lunch and to rest their weary feet.

"Do you think this sketch really and truly captures us?" Renée held up the caricature of them and studied it carefully.

"Yes," Greg replied, "it's not bad for a few minutes of work. I rather like it."

"What I like best about it," Renée interjected, "is that the artist did his rendering of us together. He captured a happiness that is ours alone. And that is what I really love."

After lunch, they went shopping along the Champs-Élysées, Avenue Victor-Hugo, and the Rue du Faubourg Saint-Honoré, one of the best areas for shopping. They went into one of the jewelry shops, and Greg chose a gold chain necklace with a love knot strung from it. "Many happy returns," Greg said as he fastened the clasp around her neck.

"Merci beaucoup, mon chéri," she said and kissed him gently on the lips. "I will cherish your gift forever."

After leaving the shop, Greg reached for his cell phone. "I'd better try reaching David back at the hotel. I wonder how he is feeling. We should share some of Paris with him. He will never forgive us if we don't."

"Greg, I was hoping you would call," David Warner exclaimed. "I tried reaching your cell phone, but it must have been turned off. I considered looking for you but then decided I'd never find you among the crowds of people."

"What is it, David?" Greg anxiously asked. "Is something wrong?"

"Your wife called almost an hour ago. Your father took a turn for the worse. She said that you had better come home as soon as possible."

Greg suddenly felt the tension rising at the back of his neck. His father had been doing very well, or so he thought. How could this have happened? Greg's mind was in turmoil. "We'll get back to the hotel right away. I am glad that I was able to reach you and get your message. Thank you so much, David."

Greg reiterated his conversation with David to Renée, and they quickly returned to the hotel. Greg made plane reservations for their trip back and quickly prepared to leave. Within a half hour, they were on their way to the airport.

"With all of this excitement," Greg said, "I completely forgot to ask about your health, David."

"I'm much better now. Thanks, Greg. Did you enjoy Paris?"

"Oh we loved it," Renée responded. "It was a perfect day. I wish it hadn't ended so abruptly."

"Yes," Greg replied, "you'll just have to see it another time, Dave. There will be other trips back, I guarantee it."

Looking out of the window, David caught a quick glimpse of the city of Paris as the cab sped toward the airport. "On my next trip, I will have to bring my wife along. She would love to see Paris."

Greg felt as if he had been reprimanded. He had not considered bringing Vanessa along on this trip. It had been a rather extraordinary time for him, and he wished that this day could have lasted an eternity. He was given the opportunity to fully experience the renewal of grand passion unleashed and intense with Renée. He remembered the softness of her body against his and the warmth of her lips touching his. The tremendous pleasure and exhilaration of making love to such a voluptuous woman remained in his senses. It was an exciting and unique experience, he thought, one that would have to last him a lifetime.

Greg, Renée, and David boarded the plane and very soon were airborne and on their way back home. They indulged in very little conversation. Instead, each one retreated into their own private thoughts.

Chapter 14

Greg quickly walked down the hallway toward his father's hospital room. He saw his wife standing outside the door, appearing very morose and staring at the floor. As Greg approached, Vanessa looked up at her husband, blinking away the tears that were filling her eyes.

How vulnerable she looked, Greg thought, yet he could not bring himself to take her in his arms to comfort her. It was too soon after he had held another woman in his arms, and the memory of her touch still lingered. "How's Dad doing? Has there been any change?"

"He's not doing well at all, Greg. He seems to be failing rapidly. Dr. Brooks is in there with him now."

"Where is Mother? Is she in Dad's room?" Greg asked.

"Yes, Dr. Brooks allowed her to remain in the room. There she is now."

Lenore walked out of Mac's room, weeping. "He doesn't know me anymore. He's completely given up. I feel so helpless watching him slipping away from me."

Greg passed his mother and quickly made his way to his father's side. Dr. Brooks was standing over Mac, trying to wake him, but there was no response. A nurse checked the intravenous fluid that was emptying into Mac's veins. Greg stared at his father, watching him breathe, his chest rising and lowering in shallow but rhythmic motion.

Dr. Brooks walked out of the room to speak with Lenore and also to Melanie, who had just arrived. "He should not have rejected Dr. Ulrich's study. This is very unfortunate."

Mac slept serenely in his last moments. Death began to take on definite features. With complete resignation, he succumbed to the calling of this form of life. He ceased to breathe and was finally at peace.

Greg quickly summoned Dr. Brooks back into the room, but there was nothing that anyone could have done. Mac was gone. Only the shell of the man remained. The spirit had left to begin its new life.

Greg took his mother and held her as she wept in his arms. They stood together, locked in overwhelming sorrow, unable to speak.

Dr. Brooks took Melanie and comforted her. "Your father wanted it this way, Melanie. He no longer put up a fight to live. He died very peacefully in his sleep. We should be grateful for that."

Melanie brushed away the tears from her face as she looked up at him. "I simply can't believe it. Never for a moment did I think we would lose him. I loved him so much, Richard."

He held her closely in his arms, feeling the sobbing coming in waves. "I know, Melanie, I know. It will be a difficult adjustment to make, but you will be just fine."

Melanie was not a woman who cried easily, but the next few days were going to be emotionally draining. She could not promise to be strong nor brave for her mother's sake, for her boys, or even for herself.

The following days did prove to be very distressing for the entire family. Lenore held up relatively well during the funeral. But after it was over, she wept with a bursting relief from the grief, which, up till now, she held in check.

Lenore felt a dreadful loss and an overwhelming desolation. She had lost a man who meant more to her than life itself. He had been more than a husband to her, especially during the last few years. He had been her dearest companion. They had always been good for each other during all the years of their marriage. Now he was gone, and she felt that a part of her had gone with him. It almost made her feel off-balance. She had to pick up the pieces of her life and get on with it again. After all, she did have her children and grandchildren to think of, and they would always fill up her life.

*　*　*

Several days later, the family was summoned for the reading of the last will and testament of MacGregor Stone to be held in the offices of Trent, Randolph, and Lambert.

Rain had been threatening for days, and it finally arrived. It came down in torrents, as if the sky had opened up and was shedding a multitude of tears.

Alan Lambert sat at his desk and read the will to Lenore and her two adult children, Greg and Melanie. He explained Mac's bequests and stipulations. After the reading was over, Alan pulled out an envelope that had been included with the will. He handed it to Greg and instructed him to read it.

Greg looked rather puzzled as he accepted the envelope. He felt apprehensive as he ripped it open and pulled out the contents. His hands shook somewhat as he slowly unfolded the letter. After a moment, he began to read aloud.

To my beloved wife, Lenore,

> *I think you know that I have always loved you with all of my heart and soul. Neither chance nor time, not even death, can change that love. You have always been most important to me, even if at times I was too busy to tell you. I hope that you have known it. You have been patient and wonderful through all of our life together and even during my illness. I sincerely hope and pray that you will not think any less of me after the conclusion of this letter.*

A PRECIOUS COMMODITY

To my dear son, Greg, and my loving daughter, Melanie,

I have always been very proud of both of you and your many accomplishments. Greg, I know that your plans for the company are somewhat more progressive than mine have been lately, but truly, I am pleased. This is the time for a new beginning and a fresh approach. You have proven your desire and ability to accomplish this. The company has been placed in very capable hands to continue with its progression.

Melanie, thank you for being the best daughter a father could have. You have been loving and generous with your time. Your artistic talent and your good sense of humor have been an anodyne when I felt low. I would like to thank you both for making your mother and me the happiest grandparents ever by bestowing upon us three very wonderful grandchildren. You have done an excellent job with them. You should be proud.

Greg, I have a request to make of you. My age has earned for me the right to be a doting father. It would please me if the company would continue to remain within the family from generation to generation. I would also like your mother to be on the board of directors. She understands the business as well as I do. We had always discussed everything together, every accomplishment and every aspect. This will give her something to do and keep her out of mischief. These are my wishes that I would like to be carried out. However, one in my position can merely try to be persuasive. No, that word is not strong enough. I think we are back to doting again. I suspect that word will be included in my epitaph.

Finally, I must reveal something that is a matter of conscience. If I may borrow the words of a well-known statesman and patriot who once said, "Give me liberty or give me death." Since I cannot be liberated from my own conscience, I must therefore accept the alternative.

Several months ago, my stepbrother, Ivan, discovered a new drug that proved to be somewhat of a miracle. After some extensive testing, the drug proved most effective on leukemia. However, it also worked well on other forms of malignancies and didn't have the dreadful toxic side effects as do the other chemotherapeutic agents on the market. Manufacture of the drug had not yet commenced when Ivan received a request to destroy the formula, and a threat on his life was made if he did not do as he was told. Somehow, the information about the new drug had leaked out. The source of which, I do not know. However, in spite of the request, preparation for the manufacture of the drug had begun. This is what seemed to bring on threats that had all the earmarks of being life threatening to the rest of the family, particularly being concentrated on a most vulnerable member, my granddaughter, Marissa. She was being closely scrutinized, making it obvious to me that she could very easily become a victim of this unknown pursuer. This had become increasingly evident with the procurement of her ruby ring, so skillfully implemented by this iniquitous entity. Becoming fearful for Marissa's safety, I had ordered the ceasing of production of the drug.

How ironic it was that I should have become inflicted with the very disease for which there now existed a complete and indefinite remission, if not a complete cure. Since it was my decision to keep the drug from being distributed, I took upon my conscience all those innocent people and so many children who have died because of my decision. As retribution for my lack of courage, I chose not to take the medication and sacrifice my life in return for the innocent victims of a disease that I had the ability to cure. Unfortunately, even in death, I shall not rest in peace until the culprit who threatened the lives of my family has been discovered, along with his informer, an obvious leak within our own company.

This conspiracy must be stopped, and the drug must be put on the market to end the insidious destruction of lives.

Enclosed are some of the threatening notes that I, as well as Ivan have received. The notes might, very well, help in the investigation. Hopefully this criminal and his accomplice, if any, will be discovered and justice be served. I leave you all with this enormous task.

With all my love and unceasing devotion,

Mac

As Greg completed reading the letter, a most dreadful anger surfaced in him; the likes of which he had not experienced before. His face took on a crimson red hue as he read through the threat notes that were enclosed in the letter.

"He willed himself to die to appease his conscience," Greg declared, "when all along he held the cure but chose deliberately not to take it." Greg looked up with exasperation on his face. "What gave him the right to wield all of this power? Did he think he was God! Why wasn't I told about the formula?" Greg was practically shouting at this point.

Lenore studied her son through tear-filled eyes but remained silent. To her, Mac's decision only meant extreme bravery and total selflessness. Her admiration for her husband was seconded only by the grief she was feeling over his loss. Her life would never be the same without him. Mac had always been the essence of her being. Now, he was gone, and she would have to find new meaning and purpose to her life. She knew that it would be a difficult road.

Melanie rose from her chair and walked over to her brother's side.

"May I see those notes, Greg?"

He handed them to her, still feeling the terrible anger inside.

"So this is what all of the secrets have been about." She examined the notes very carefully. There was something familiar about them, but she simply could not figure out what that could be at this point. It was all too shocking to absorb just yet. She was going to mull it over until she had the answer.

Greg continued to skim over his father's letter. In spite of his anger, Greg admired his father's enormous courage and fortitude. For the first time in his life, Greg felt that he truly and completely understood him. However, it was unfortunate that only in death was he able to accomplish this. The anger he felt was due to the senseless loss because of someone else's selfish motives. He wondered what could have driven someone to prevent the manufacture of this most wonderful medication that would save countless lives. He must have had something to gain by it. Only someone truly depraved could have been guilty of such a heinous crime.

"I am going to find out who had cost Father's life," Greg said. "And I fully intend to go on with the manufacture and distribution of the medication. To hell with the threats!"

Later, as Greg returned home, his anger had reached profound depths. He had the entire long and tedious drive home in the pouring rain to ponder upon the most current revelations in his father's letter. In the car, Vanessa had made several attempts at evoking a conversation, but it was to no avail.

Greg had decided to take action immediately. This was the time for a new beginning. The past would be washed away. As the pouring rain cleared away everything in its path, he too would rid himself of the obstacles that held him back, and he would avenge his father's death. Nothing would hold him back.

As soon as he reached home, Greg dialed Ivan's number and waited for him to answer. "Ivan, this is Greg. I've just read the letter which had been left by my father revealing the news of the formula and all of the incidents connected with it, including the reason for his death."

"I knew about the letter, Greg, and about everything else. There was no way that I could change his mind. I tried to convince him to let me administer the medication to him, but he refused time and again. He felt that he did not have the right. Allowing himself to suffer and die was a just punishment for his crime of omission. Your father was very altruistic and very strong willed. I could not go against his wishes. He was my stepbrother, and I loved him dearly. It was very painful to watch him suffer and die when he could have been saved."

"I know, I know, Ivan." For a moment, Greg forgot the purpose of his phone call. His deep sadness returned, and his anger was gone. He had to collect his thoughts once more and push back the sorrow that loomed over him. "I want to see that formula, Ivan. Do you have it in your possession now?"

"Yes, I have kept it in my safe at home. Just recently, someone had ransacked my office at the lab, apparently in search of the formula. Luckily, I did not keep it there. No doubt it would have been found at that time if I had. I also felt that someone had entered my home as well, but fortunately, was not able to steal the formula from my locked safe. If you wish to see it, I will bring it over tomorrow."

"No, Ivan, I must see it now. I want you to bring it to my home tonight. I must see it immediately!" Greg's anger returned along with his impatience and an urgency that had to be fulfilled.

"All right, Greg, I will be there with the formula this evening."

Greg hung up the phone and paced back and forth with renewed and unrestrained vigor, occasionally looking out of the window at the rain pounding against the glass, coming down in torrents.

Chapter 15

Alan Lambert sat quietly in his study, going over some briefs at his desk for the following day. A moment later, there was a soft knock on the door, and Melanie walked in.

"I didn't want to disturb you, Alan," she said. "But I need the letters that I had left on the desk earlier. They have to be mailed tomorrow the latest, and I still need to enclose some information about the art gallery."

Alan looked over on the desk and saw the letters. "Yes, of course, honey, come on in."

Melanie took the letters and checked them over quickly. She then began to search around the desk, looking through the papers that were neatly stacked at one end. Not being able to find what she was searching for, Melanie began going through the drawers.

"Melanie, what are you looking for? You're disturbing my train of thought. I have to finish reading these briefs for tomorrow." Alan had a rather curt edge to his voice as he spoke. He then picked up a small stack of papers that he had earlier cast aside. "Is this what you are looking for?"

"Oh yes! I'm so glad you found them. I was beginning to get worried. They are very important. There's going to be a fund-raising dinner for the art gallery. We are going to have some brochures printed with information about the art auction, as well as some information about the art gallery itself. They will be distributed at the dinner. The secretary is in charge of the printing, so I'm forwarding the info to her."

"Well, now you're all set," Alan replied.

"Only temporarily," Melanie interjected, opening a small top drawer. "I have more writing to do as soon as you vacate this desk."

Alan noticed her rummaging through the drawer. "What are you looking for now?"

"Envelopes, I need envelopes to mail out the invitations. Once I get those addressed, most of my work will be complete." Finally coming across them, she announced, "Now I'll leave you to your work. My work will have to wait till later. I'll go upstairs to say good night to the boys."

"Say good night to them for me as well," Alan interjected. "I won't have time to do it myself. Mark and Derek always have something to tell me about their day before going to sleep. Please be my mediator this time."

"Will do," Melanie responded and then walked toward the door. "It certainly is a rainy night. I'm so glad that we're spending the evening at home."

"Yes, so am I," Alan replied as he glanced in the direction of the large windows. "I wouldn't want to be out on a night like this."

* * *

Ivan sped down the rain-slicked highway in the direction of the Stone house. He felt relieved that everything was out in the open. By nature, he was an honest, open, and sincere person. It went against his grain to have to behave in a surreptitious manner. Ever since his experiments led to the discovery of the formula, his life had become very complicated. He wished that he could have convinced Mac to take the miraculous cure for his disease. He would have been alive today. There was even a possibility that Dr. Dan Ulrich may have kept Mac in remission with his experimental drug. But Mac refused everything that was offered to him in the form of a cure. He had made his decision to give up his life, and no one could have swayed him.

Just then, Ivan reached a bridge that was narrow and darkened due to power failure caused by the rainstorm. It was difficult for him to see the road and its parameters. The wipers could not clear the windshield fast enough from the heavy downpour.

From out of the darkness in the opposite direction, he caught a glimpse of a black truck, and it seemed to be speeding directly toward him. Ivan was almost through the narrow bridge, so he picked up speed to quickly reach the end. As he pressed his foot down on the accelerator, the truck seemed to hasten its speed as well in his direction, crossing the double yellow line that divided the road. Ivan swerved sharply to the right in an effort to avoid colliding with the truck. At that moment, he reached the end of the bridge only to find that there was an opening in the guardrail. The car reached the edge of the precipice. Ivan applied his brakes, but his car slipped in the mud and glided smoothly over. For a moment, it was airborne, but then it tumbled over and over, amassing rock and soil, and burst into flames at the bottom of the cliff.

Chapter 16

Lenore sorted through Mac's things, and the memories of the wonderful years they shared together swept over her as they did many times ever since he passed away. Each article of clothing, his gold watch and cuff links and his colognes, stirred in her the strong emotions she felt for him. His loss left an empty chamber in her heart that would devastate her for years to come, possibly for the rest of her life.

She sat down on the bed with the watch in her hand and read the inscription on the back, "Chance cannot change my love nor time impair." Lenore had given the watch to Mac for their twenty-fifth wedding anniversary and had chosen for the inscription a quote from her favorite poet, Elizabeth Barrett Browning.

She remembered the look of overwhelming surprise on Mac's face as he opened the small box. It had given him so much pleasure, and from that moment on, he rarely went anywhere without it. To him, it was a constant reminder of his good fortune to have married such a wonderful and loving woman.

Time was on their side then; they were to have twenty more years together. Their children were grown. Greg was twenty-two, and Melanie was seventeen. The pharmaceutical company to which Mac had devoted so much time and energy was now successfully profitable. At that point in their lives, everything was on the upswing. Lenore wished that she could physically return to that time, but of course, that was merely a paradoxical vision. She had to go forward—no matter how difficult it was going to be.

The holiday season would be here in a few short months. The entire family would be together, with the exception of a very important member. Lenore would feel the emptiness of not having Mac at her side. She felt as if she had suffered a loss of a limb from her body. She felt terribly incomplete and had to learn to cope with life again. It was a dreadful feeling of inadequacy, like being left at the edge of a dark, narrow ledge and having to find her way back alone.

Lenore experienced a tinge of fear grasp at her as the muscles in her neck began to tense. She put her hand to her neck and began massaging it but knew that the tension would not leave her unless she busied herself with some kind of routine.

Mac had always wanted her to take an interest in the company. He spoke to her on numerous occasions of the structure and the occasional problems that required solving. She had been his sounding board, but more than that, she had often given him constructive advice, which he would implement. However, Lenore never actively participated in the business. Now she intended to give Mac his wish and finally get involved. It would be a challenge but would serve a two-fold purpose. Lenore knew it would please him and would also keep her occupied enough to get her through this very difficult time.

What intense pride she felt in her husband's courage while he was ill. She, of course, was aware of her husband's enormous strength of character but never realized the full extent of it before.

* * *

An hour had passed since Greg had spoken to Ivan. The rain had finally let up and whirled away with the spirals of intense wind. The tumultuous dark clouds disappeared and allowed the stars to glitter through.

Greg paced the floor impatiently, glancing with an irascible eye toward the large Georgian grandfather clock that chimed the eleventh hour. He walked to the telephone, wondering what was keeping Ivan. *It should not be taking him this long to get here*, he thought. *Where is he*? As he reached to pick up the phone to call Ivan's cell phone, he was startled by its sudden ringing. "Hello!" Greg shouted his anxiety apparent in his voice.

"Hello, this is Sergeant Halstead of the police department. I'd like to speak to Greg Stone please."

Greg felt the tension rising and his heartbeat quicken. "Speaking," he said. "Is something wrong?"

"Do you know an Ivan Kerensky, sir?"

"Yes, I do. Where is he?"

"I'm afraid, Mr. Stone, that he's been in an accident. His car went off the road and down an embankment. He was thrown clear as the car exploded into flames at the bottom. Just before he died, he mentioned your name, and that's why you have been notified. I'd like you to come down to the morgue and identify the body. Tomorrow, first thing in the morning, will be fine, Mr. Stone. I'm sorry to have to give you this news."

Greg could not speak for a moment. This new shock was creating resounding reverberations against his sternum. After all that his family had been through, now this has happened.

"I'm very grateful that you did call, Sergeant Halstead, and of course, I will be there to identify the body tomorrow. Where did the accident occur?"

Greg began to wonder about the formula. Questions began to torment him. Was the formula lying around somewhere near the scene of the accident for anyone to get hold of it? Had it been destroyed by the fire and forever lost?

Sergeant Halstead told Greg the location of the accident, which was just a couple of miles down the road from the Stone house.

"Thank you, Sergeant Halstead, for notifying me."

Greg hung up the phone, grabbed his raincoat, and dashed out of the house. As he turned the ignition key of his car, he remembered hearing sirens from an emergency vehicle in the distance during his anticipated wait for Ivan's arrival earlier in the evening. His mind raced in all directions with the burgeoning fear of losing the formula along with the man who had discovered it. What a monstrous waste, he thought, as he sped toward the scene of the dreadful accident.

As he approached the scene of the accident, Greg noticed that the remains of the burned-out car had just been hauled out of the ravine and was being prepared to be taken away. He walked out to one of the policemen who was making an observation of the skid marks on the road.

"Hello, I'm Greg Stone. I'm related to the man who was killed in this accident. Mind if I have a look around?"

He looked up at Greg. "Yes, Mr. Stone, you can look around all you like. We're practically finished here, except for this other set of tire marks that seem to swerve toward the opposite side of the road and then pull back. It appears to me that this other car was responsible for Kerensky's accident."

Greg took a closer look at the double set of tire tracks. "You know, you could, very well, be right about that. It certainly does look as if Ivan's car was forced off the road right here."

"I'd say it was probably a truck, judging from the wide wheelbase and the tire size. From the close proximity of the two sets of tire tracks, the vehicles just may have scraped together. That, in itself, might give us a lead." The police officer looked squarely at Greg. "Would you happen to know where this Ivan was going in a rainstorm? And do you know if there was any reason why someone would want to kill him?"

Greg pondered a moment, wondering how much to tell the police officer. If the formula had not been destroyed in the explosion, he didn't want anyone else to find it. It was extremely valuable to him, both personally and monetarily. He did not want it to get into the wrong hands. He had to find it, if it was still around. Someone had been after Ivan, it appeared, and might possibly have caused his death. Who was this culprit, this murderer, who came out on a rainy night and forced Ivan off the road to his death? Greg had to get to the bottom of this. After all, even his daughter's life was being threatened. If the formula was gone, maybe it would all stop. But he had to know who was responsible for this corruption.

"Mr. Stone, I asked you, do you know of anyone who wanted Ivan Kerensky dead?" He looked at Greg rather strangely in anticipation of his answer.

Greg gathered his thoughts quickly. "Oh, I'm sorry, Officer. This entire thing is very upsetting. No, I haven't any idea who might have wanted Ivan dead. I wish I did, believe me. Now, if you don't mind, I'd like to look around a bit."

"Sure, Mr. Stone, go right ahead. If you find anything unusual, let us know." He turned and walked over to the patrol car with its flashing lights to make a report on his radio. He then left the scene of the accident.

Greg combed the area where the car left the road and continued downward to where it tumbled over and exploded. The ground was drenched and slippery from the rain as he descended the steep embankment. His shoes became caked with mud, and the bottoms of his pants were spattered and mucky as he rummaged around in the dark. There was no trace of the formula anywhere. As Greg climbed back up to the road, he caught the glimmer of something metal lying in the mud just a few feet away. He picked it up and examined it. The object appeared to be a piece of chrome stripping. As he slipped it into his pocket, he wondered if it belonged to the truck that might have been there earlier that night.

Chapter 17

The following day, Greg sat in his office, unable to concentrate on his work. He had just returned from the city morgue, where he had identified the remains of his beloved uncle Ivan.

Greg was naturally feeling very introspective and allowed himself to drift into the labyrinth of his mind. He closed his eyes, shutting out the sounds coming from the outer office. A myriad of images began to form in his imagination. He saw himself and his sister, Melanie, as children spending enjoyable moments with their uncle Ivan. The memories became precision clear.

As a boy, Greg had always looked forward to his uncle's visits. He was so warm and jolly and played games with him and Melanie. He often demonstrated magic tricks to the wide-eyed amazement of the Stone children.

Ivan had, on many occasions, taken them on hikes out into the wilderness and taught them all about nature and even taught them to fish. He spent more time with them than did their own father.

What a monstrous act of violence, he thought. *Has no one any decency or even a conscience left?* All of the copies of the formula may have been destroyed in the wreckage. Ivan should have taken the precaution of leaving a copy behind. Greg felt that it would be safer with him. After all, there was the time that Ivan's lab had been broken into and obviously searched. This was, no doubt, his reasoning. He wished that he had not asked Ivan to bring the formula to his house on such a stormy night. As a result, Ivan was gone and, with him, the formula. There was no longer a miracle drug for the cure of cancer. Research had to be started all over again. What a price they all had paid.

Greg's eyes then came to rest on the photographs of his wife, Vanessa, and his daughter, Marissa, forever held in time, encased in gold and glass. *Thank God they're safe*, he thought. *There should be no more threats now that the formula is gone.* Though he wondered, what was the identity of the man who had followed Marissa and seemed to know her every move? Who, in fact, was able to get her birthstone ring, a family heirloom that once belonged to her great-grandmother? Would Marissa ever see the ring again? Who knew that Ivan would be on the road to his house with the formula last evening, and why was he so violently prevented from reaching my home?

Greg then regarded Vanessa's photograph with feelings of guilt groping after him. He wondered if she suspected what had happened while he was away in Paris, that he and Renée had made love together and had a night more passionate than he had had with her in quite some time. The grand passion had now somehow eluded them.

What was he going to do about Renée? What was so different about her that attracted him so strongly? There was a special quality about her. She possessed outward manifestations of extraordinary beauty and aggressive charm. Just thinking about her aroused him and brought back memories of her softness and warmth. Their wonderfully joyous night of intimacy would remain a memory that he would always cherish.

But he loved his wife and would never dream of hurting her. Their lives were completely interlaced and woven together. He could not envision life without her.

Interrupting his reverie, Greg's secretary buzzed the intercom. "Mr. Stone, Renée Bordeaux is here and would like just a few moments of your time."

"All right, send her in."

Renée walked in holding in check all her other emotions except grief for a man who was so well loved within the company. "Greg," she said, "I'm so sorry to hear about Ivan. How dreadful to have this happen to such a wonderful and loyal man as Ivan. We will miss him."

"Thank you, Renée. Yes, we will all miss him."

"If there is anything that I can do, please, Greg, don't hesitate to ask. You know, of course, that I would do anything for you."

Greg gazed at her and knew what she meant. Their bond was closer now than it ever had been. He knew that she expected many more nights like the one they had shared in Paris. The knowledge of this created in him shivers of delight, and he felt warmly amused. "I have already made some arrangements, and thank you again, Renée. There will be services held tomorrow for anyone who wishes to attend." He gathered the papers scattered on his desk and placed them into a folder. "I'm going to be leaving in a couple of hours, as soon as I can get a few things cleared up around here. Then I will not be back for a couple of days."

"Oh yes, I see, of course." Renée paused for a moment, collecting her thoughts and trying desperately to keep her emotions under control. "Will I be seeing you at all, Greg? I really must talk to you some time very soon."

Knowing what she was getting at, he avoided looking into her eyes. "Yes, I understand, Renée. Anything of a personal nature will have to wait for a few days, I'm afraid. My family has to come first right now. I hope that you can understand that."

"Yes, I do," Renée replied with some discomfort. *Do I have a choice*, she thought. *He will be preoccupied for some time.* Very disappointed, she turned toward the door to leave.

Feeling the necessity to change the subject, Greg quickly remarked, "I'm calling together a meeting of the executive board this morning to discuss our new facility in France. I will expect you at the meeting."

"Then I will be seeing you shortly." Renée walked out of the office, feeling a cold chill invading her body. He was rather perverse, she thought, and so coolly detached. She could not understand the dichotomy of his behavior. Was this the same man who so fervently made love to her in Paris? She hoped that his attitude toward her was colored only by the fact that the family had sustained another tragedy. She knew that it would take some time for Greg to get over Ivan's death. But of course, she would do everything in her power to help him overcome his grief within as short a period as possible.

Chapter 18

One hour later, Greg sat at the head of a long conference table before his distinguished board members and addressed them. "As most of you have probably already heard, Ivan Kerensky, our most beloved and brilliant scientist, has been killed in an automobile accident. This will prove to be a great loss to our pharmaceutical company. Several months ago, Ivan was doing some experimentation at his lab at home on white blood cells and the immune system. He discovered a drug that would destroy all cancer cells while preserving the good ones. However, last night, I asked him to bring his formula to my home. On his way over, something had happened just a short distance from my home which forced him off the road. All the police have to go on is a set of tire tracks and skid marks left by another automobile which appeared to cross the road. It apparently came toward Ivan's car just where he went down the embankment. Because of this, I have chosen to read to you a very personal letter written by my father just before he died, which I would now like you to hear."

He motioned to his recording secretary, who opened up the letter and read the last portion of it that pertained to Mac choosing to die and about the threats to the immediate family.

The board members all listened with bated breath to the revelations unfolding before them. Most of them were beginning to experience shock and disbelief. Finally, the recording secretary stopped reading, and the room was filled with low murmurs.

After a moment, Greg spoke. "So you see, what my father and Ivan thought was a carefully guarded secret was not kept confidential. I, myself, did not know about it, but someone within the company must have overheard a conversation between Ivan and my father. From my conversation with Ivan, they were the only two people who knew of the existence of the formula. However, in light of the threats, the information leaked out somehow. We will have to find out how that happened and who may have contributed to Ivan's accident and resulting death.

Greg looked down and opened a folder that he had placed directly in front of him.

"Another item on the agenda is our new facility, which we have just recently acquired in Paris. As you know, we have been planning a large expansion to foreign soil, and this was our first endeavor in that direction. We expect to broaden our base tremendously and, possibly, in the very near future.

I will be placing one of you in this room in charge of that facility. The announcement of which, I will save for a later date, till I have had some time for consideration of whom it will be. Thank you for your attention. Meeting is adjourned."

Everyone began to file out and return to their respective offices.

Renée remained behind and waited for Greg. "I'm so sorry, Greg. How dreadful it must be for you and your family. To think, your father might have been cured if he had decided to take the medication. Of course, we don't know what the fallout would have been. I wonder how much worse it would have been."

"My daughter could have also become a victim. She had been stalked, you know," Greg added.

"Yes, I did hear that, and I am so sorry. If there is anything at all that I can do, you know I'm more than willing to help in any way that I can."

Greg placed his hand on her shoulder as he spoke.

"I know, Renée, and I am very grateful. You and I are good friends."

"I like to think that we are more than just good friends. Look closer, my dear Greg. Don't you see more than just a good friend?"

Greg studied her a moment then smiled. "Yes, I see a very beautiful, loving, and generous woman. You are also a tremendous asset to this company. You are one terrific lady!"

Renée quickly glanced around to see that everyone else had left the room and the door was closed. She put her arms around him and very sensuously brought her lips to his and lingered there. "Oh, Greg, you mean everything to me," she said and then again pressed her lips to his.

He responded to her warmly. He realized how much he needed and wanted her. His resolve of a couple of hours ago had suddenly been forgotten. He felt his passion rising as he held her very closely. "I'm giving you the afternoon off, Ms. Bordeaux. We will get some lunch and then find a place where we can be alone without any interruptions. How does that sound?"

"*C'est très bien*, Greg! There is nothing I would rather do."

They drove out to the country and lunched at a lovely little restaurant noted for its delicious cuisine. All during lunch, they joked and laughed and thoroughly enjoyed each other's company. Greg was finally able to forget all of the problems that had been nagging him. However, when they finished their lunch, Renée began teasing about wanting to make love again, but Greg began to retreat back to the mystery of Ivan's death and the evidence he had collected.

"Renée, this was a wonderful and relaxing lunch, but my brain keeps reverting back to what has happened. I am very sorry, Renée, but I really need to take care of some things."

"Oh no, Greg, how can I change your mind? I know I can help you to forget your problems. Please stay," she pleaded.

"I'm so very sorry, but I must go, Renée. Maybe another time. I really need to speak to the police regarding the case."

They left the restaurant, and Greg dropped her off at work. Renée felt absolutely crushed that she could not convince Greg to stay and spend the afternoon with her.

Greg had gone to meet with Sergeant Halstead to give him the piece of metal that he had found at the crash site as possible evidence. He hoped that it would help to identify the truck that had sent Ivan's car over the precipice. It, of course, would be a difficult task since the truck could belong to anyone. He also needed to give the threat notes that were enclosed in his father's will. They were meant to prevent the manufacture of the anticancer drug that Ivan had discovered with a threat to the family. Marissa could be put in danger, as shown by the accessibility to her and by the easy acquirement of her ring.

Chapter 19

The following day, after the services for Ivan had been held, Greg left for Ivan's town house in search of some possible clues of any kind and also for some notes he may have left behind pertaining to the formula or possibly even an extra copy.

In a desk drawer, Greg found a few scribbled notes and calculations that he thought might be pertinent. He put them into his pocket, hoping that one of the other scientists on his staff might be able to decipher them, that is, if the notes had anything at all to do with the secret formula. In his haste, he suddenly knocked the handset off the phone base. As he reached to pick it up, something occurred to him. Did someone overhear his last conversation with Ivan? How else would anyone have known that Ivan would be on his way to Greg's house the night he was killed? Someone had broken into Ivan's lab as well as his home. Did someone tap his phone? When did someone have the opportunity to do this? Greg quickly picked up the handset and, to his amazement, found a very small microphone inside. "So it was bugged!" he said aloud. He would have to tell the police about this new evidence. He then combed through the rest of the house in search of anything else that might be significant. He was careful to wear plastic gloves while doing his search in case there were fingerprints left by the intruder. Sergeant Halstead's group went through the house before for any kind of evidence but had not found the small microphone.

When he returned home, Greg continued to mull over all the evidence that he had found. He recalled Marissa's missing ring, the threat notes, and the description of the man who had been stalking Marissa. He was tall, middle-aged, had brown hair streaked with gray, wore a baseball cap and sunglasses, and had a chipped front tooth.

Then it suddenly occurred to him that other phones may have been tapped. He quickly checked the phone on his desk and found no microphone. He then raced through the house, checking the other phones. He found no evidence of any taps.

Hearing all the commotion, Vanessa came out of the kitchen, where she had been preparing to bake an apple pie. "Greg, I hadn't realized you were home. What on earth are you doing?"

"I'm just checking our phones for tapping devices. I went to Ivan's house to have a look around, and quite by accident, I discovered that his phone had a small microphone in it. Naturally, I began to suspect that other phones may have been bugged as well."

There was a look of alarm on Vanessa's face. "My God, when will there be an end to all of this?"

"Not till I find out who's behind it all. Ivan may have been killed for that formula. Someone overheard our conversation that night before his accident. Whoever it is knew that he was on his way to see me and prevented him from getting here. In the process, the formula was destroyed, so it served a two-fold purpose. It all makes sense."

"Greg, I would just like to forget all about this and let us lead normal lives again. I'm sure, now that the formula is gone and its creator, Marissa won't be threatened anymore. If you begin to stir things up, who knows what will happen. Greg, please leave it alone. Let the police handle it. It's their job."

Greg went up to Vanessa and kissed her tenderly for the first time since he came back from Paris. She seemed so terribly vulnerable, and this is what appealed to his masculine strength. He comforted her but could not promise to stop his investigation. "The police are looking for the truck which may have pushed Ivan's car over the cliff. You've read the papers, honey. They are looking for witnesses who might have seen anything unusual that night down the road."

"Did you find anything else at Ivan's? Was there another copy of the formula anywhere?" Vanessa inquired.

"No, Van, I'm afraid not, but I did find a few papers in his desk that might have something to do with the formula. I will show them to one of the scientists in the lab. Hopefully, it will be found that the papers contain pertinent information on the formula."

"What about the threat notes?" Vanessa asked. "Do you know who the author could be?"

"No, I don't know, but I intend to find out. I'm going to check out a few more phones for tapping devices. I wish to God that I would have thought to do this before Ivan was killed. It might not have happened."

"Don't blame yourself, Greg. Whoever wanted Ivan and his formula destroyed would have found another way. No one could have prevented it," replied Vanessa. "There wasn't enough time. You found out about the existence of the formula the same day that Ivan was killed. Your father said in his letter that it was a conspiracy, that this person had at least one accomplice. There may be several people involved."

"You know, Van, the more conspirators involved in the plot, the easier it will be for one of them to make a mistake. As you know, I already have some of the evidence."

"Well, my dear husband, even though I think you are brilliant, I still feel that you should just turn everything over to the police and let them handle it. You are the president of a pharmaceutical company, not a detective."

"I have been doing just that, but I can't simply sit back and do nothing. Van, I owe it to my dad, as well as to Ivan, to get to the bottom of this. I suspected that something strange was going on for quite some time, but I wasn't able to prove anything. It was merely a gut feeling that turned out to be right."

Vanessa got out of the chair in which she was sitting. "Well, I'll leave you to your investigation, Sherlock. Dinner is almost ready, and you should see the dessert we are having! It's just going to be the two of us tonight. Marissa is going out with Paul Glasser."

"Is she still seeing that intern?"

"Yes, I am, Daddy," Marissa replied as she descended the stairs. "Do you have any objections?"

Greg looked up at his lovely daughter and felt a sense of fatherly pride and admiration.

"No, baby, I haven't. He seems smart enough to know that he has a real gem of a girl. And knowing that, I think he treats you well. Am I right?"

"He is always polite, and we always have a good time together. Don't worry Dad, we're just good friends."

"That's just what a father likes to hear," Greg replied with a broad grin.

Outside, Paul Glasser pulled into the driveway of the Stone house with his rather noisy sports car. He hopped out and briskly walked to the front door. Almost as soon as he rang the doorbell, Marissa opened the door.

"Hi, Paul, you are always so prompt."

Paul felt pleased and gave Marissa a warm smile. "Well then, I guess that makes two of us. You are always ready when I arrive."

As they walked into the living room, Greg looked up from the newspaper he had begun to read. "Hello, Paul, how are you?"

"Just fine, sir, and you?"

"Oh not bad," replied Greg warmly. "Where are you taking my daughter this evening?"

"We're going to the new restaurant that just opened up at the edge of town. My friends tell me that the food is very good and so is the atmosphere."

Just then, Vanessa walked into the room. "I thought I heard the doorbell ring a minute go. Hello, Paul!"

"Hello, Mrs. Stone," Paul replied. "I smell something terrific cooking."

"We're having a pork loin roast with a maple glaze, and you are welcome to stay. There is plenty of food to go around."

"Thanks, but not this time, Mrs. Stone. We already have reservations for dinner, but I certainly will take a rain check."

"Have a good time, you kids," Greg interjected. "And don't be out too late."

"Don't worry, Mr. Stone, Marissa will be home at a reasonable time."

The young couple left the house and headed for the car parked outside in the driveway. Greg watched as they climbed in, and the car backed out and pulled away.

Vanessa began to bring the food out into the dining room. The room was glowing with candlelight, and the table was set for two. "Come on, Greg, sit down. Dinner is served."

Greg turned to admire the elegant display. "Hmm, everything looks terrific." He walked over to the table and sat down. "Looking out the window just then, I was simply remembering how it was when we were dating. But I don't believe that my car was as loud as Paul's."

Vanessa joined him at the table and listened with amusement. "No, I don't think that it was. You were a little more conservative. Paul seems like a nice young man. I don't mind Marissa dating him."

"Well, she is in college now, and I don't think that we will have anything to say about whom she dates much longer, do you?" Greg questioned.

"No, I suppose not," she replied.

After indulging in their delicious repast, Greg helped Vanessa clear the table. When they had completed putting all the dishes in the dishwasher, Vanessa came up to Greg and, cupping his face in her hands, she planted a grateful kiss squarely on his lips. "That's for being such a gem yourself and helping me with the dishes."

Greg laughed with amusement. "I did it because I love you. You know, Van, I really do love you."

"I'd like to see you prove that," Vanessa bantered impishly. For the first time in weeks, she felt an unrelenting physical need for closeness with him. Their relationship had been strained for quite some time. Greg had been spending a lot of time working. When he was with her, he seemed so terribly preoccupied, making her feel left out of his life. Their family had been through a great deal lately, so his almost indifference to her seemed somewhat natural. She could not help but feel some resentment. Tonight, things seemed better than ever, and Vanessa wanted to revel in his delightful change of mood.

Greg took Vanessa in his arms and continued the banter. "Are you trying to seduce me, young lady?"

"Well, I certainly hope so," she replied, putting her arms around him more tightly. "Did you think the apple pie was the only dessert I was talking about?"

Greg kissed her tenderly and then led her toward the stairs that led to their bedroom. "Well, you certainly had this all figured out."

As they climbed the stairs, Vanessa asked, "When are you going to tell me about your trip to Paris? You haven't mentioned a word about it."

"It can wait," said Greg. "I will tell you about it some other time."

Chapter 20

The following day, Greg went to the hospital. He had a hunch that if his father's phone had been tapped, there might be some telltale signs on the phone itself. There was also the possibility that the device might still be intact inside the phone.

When Greg reached the fourth floor, he walked up to the nurses' station and spoke to the charge nurse. "Is anyone occupying room 421?"

"No, Mr. Stone. Your dad was in that room. Are you looking for something specific? There is no one occupying the room as yet."

"If I may, I would like to check on the phone in his room. This might seem a rather unusual request, but believe me, I have a very good reason for asking."

The nurse looked at Greg questioningly. "This is highly irregular, but I suppose there is no harm in it. Come with me, Mr. Stone." The nurse motioned to Greg, and he followed her down the hall to room 421. "There is the phone. You can examine it if you like."

Greg walked over to the phone and lifted the handset. There appeared to be some scratch marks. He quickly opened it up, and inside, he found a small microphone still intact. "This is what I was looking for. You see, someone had planted this in the phone while my father was occupying this room. The police will have to check the phone and take the microphone as evidence. Please do not put another patient in this room until the police do their investigation."

"Oh my, that is pretty serious. I will make sure that no other patient occupies this room until after the police have a chance to investigate."

"Two men who were very dear to me have died, my father and uncle. There seems to be a mystery surrounding their deaths, and I'd like to get to the bottom of it." Greg did not want to alarm the nurse, so he avoided giving her too many details.

As Greg walked out of the room, he encountered Dr. Paul Glasser walking in their direction. "Hello, Mr. Stone, are you visiting one of the patients?"

"No, Paul, not exactly. But could I talk to you for a moment?"

"Sure, Mr. Stone, there's a lounge area just down the hall."

They walked to the lounge and sat down in chairs that were adjacent to each other. Greg spoke first. "It seems rather easy for anyone to walk into a patient's room unnoticed. While my father was a patient here, did you ever see anyone behaving suspiciously hanging around his room or, in fact, entering it?"

Paul looked puzzled with a suggestion of lines etching his brow. He hesitated for a moment and then answered. "No, not that I recall, Mr. Stone. The only people I noticed around his room were doctors, nurses, other hospital personnel, and, of course, his family. Why do you ask?"

Greg looked away for a moment, wondering how much information to divulge. "I found a bugging device in the phone in my father's room."

There was a rather stunned expression on Paul's face, which quickly gave way to one of scrutiny. "What makes you think that it was meant for your father and not for some previous patient? Who knows how long it has been in place."

"Because I found the exact same kind of device in Ivan's home phone the day after he died. I think there is a connection," Greg replied.

"Well, Mr. Stone, I'm sorry, but I can't help you. And like you said, it is easy for someone to walk into a patient's room unnoticed, especially if all the nurses are busy. To make it more secure, we would have to install cameras in every room. Up until now, that has not proven to be necessary."

"That is true, Paul, but this is a new problem that has probably never been encountered before. I will be giving this information over to the police. They are experienced in these matters. I'm not."

"Well, you know best. But now, I have to get back to work. Let me know how everything turns out, Mr. Stone."

Paul walked down the hall, passed the nurses' station, and turned the corner. Greg then walked down the same hallway, which also led to the elevators. Paul stopped to use his cell phone, and Greg walked into the elevator. In a minute, he was in the downstairs lobby and was walking out the door. As he did, Greg suddenly heard a familiar voice call out his name. He turned around to find Dr. Richard Brooks walking toward him.

"Hey, Greg, what's your hurry?"

"I'm on my way to the police station."

"That sounds pretty serious, Greg. Want to tell your old buddy all about it over lunch?"

"Yes, I guess so," Greg relented. "I'll use you as a sounding board. In fact, you could be a big help to me."

"Well, I certainly hope so. I would hate to let you down in what seems like a bit of a crisis."

They walked together through a maze of cars in the parking garage. Greg began to relate to his good friend the evidence he had about Ivan's death. As they stopped by Richard's car, Greg looked over and noticed that immediately next to it was a black truck that had a long scratch on the front fender and a piece of metal trim missing from the side of the truck. As he wrote the license number down, Greg asked, "Have you any idea whose truck this is? This could be the truck that forced Ivan off the road." He examined the scratch on the fender and saw brown paint that had been scraped off another vehicle. Greg then pointed to the scratch for Richard to observe. "Ivan's car was brown. I have to find out whose truck this is."

Richard looked pensive. "Wish I knew, Greg. The truck was already here when I arrived, so I didn't see the driver."

"Unfortunately, the doors are locked," Greg observed. "Otherwise, I would check the glove compartment for the registration. Well, there are other ways of finding out the name of the owner, like the number on the license plate."

"Right," Richard urged, "now let's go to lunch. I'm famished!"

They chose a restaurant a couple of blocks away from the hospital. It was convenient and was also noted for its consistent good quality of food. While the two men enjoyed their lunch, Greg continued to discuss all of his findings and also gave Richard the gist of his father's letter that had been enclosed with the will along with the threat notes.

Richard took this all in, and a troubled expression became evident on his face. "Well, the police are in a better position to find out who is behind all of this. Do Melanie and your mother know about the information you have?"

"Well, they know some of it but not everything. Why do you ask?"

"Knowing too much could be rather disconcerting," Richard acknowledged. "Have the threats stopped?"

"Yes, everything has stopped since Ivan's death."

"Glad to hear it, Greg. Say, how is Melanie? I haven't seen her lately."

"Tell me honestly, do you still have this thing for Melanie?" Greg asked, looking rather amused.

"Honestly, yes, I guess I always will. I should have done something about it years ago when I had the opportunity."

Greg studied his friend for a moment and then made an observation. "Sounds like you are suffering from a bad case of unrequited love."

"That sounds like a line from an old Victorian novel," Richard retorted.

"Why don't you come over to the house on Saturday evening, Richard? My mother, Melanie, and her husband, Alan, have been invited too. It's just a small dinner party. I'm sure you will find it interesting."

"Sure, I'll be glad to come. Thanks for the invitation."

After lunch, Richard headed back to the hospital. Greg left for the police station to speak with Sergeant Halstead regarding the metal strip he had found at the scene of Ivan's crash. He also wanted him to check the owner's identity with the license plate number of the black truck along with the long scratch marks and brown paint left behind. He also told him his other evidence regarding the wiretaps in Mac's hospital room as well as Ivan's home. In addition, he released to Sergeant Halstead the threat notes that were enclosed in Mac's letter. He felt relieved to part with all the evidence he had gathered but was also rather enthused about his investigation and hoped to solve Ivan's murder.

Sergeant Halstead listened to Greg's report of the evidence he had and was inspired by the fact that he had been delving into this case with such intensity. "I am amazed that you have given me more to go on than anyone in the department has been able to uncover. How would you like a side job of being a consultant to the police department? We could certainly use someone like you who has such dogged commitment to the task. Of course, I realize that you have a vested interest in this particular case since it involves your family member. But maybe you could inspire some of the people around here to do a better job of investigation."

Greg appeared rather amused at Sergeant Halstead's request. "Thank you for the confidence and, in fact, the praise, but I do have a large business to run. This could be an interesting hobby, but that is all it could be, especially at this point in time."

"Okay then, Mr. Stone, we will check out the wiretaps for fingerprints and get the name of the owner of that vehicle to see if there is a connection with the accident or, very possibly, a crime. I will keep in touch with you and relate any info that we get. Thanks, Mr. Stone, and hopefully, this case will soon be solved. If you change your mind about doing some sleuthing for us, we could certainly use your help. It could be interesting for you whenever you do have the time."

"I will keep it in mind. You could be right about that," Greg replied. "Right now though, I have to leave for my office. There is a lot to be done." Greg walked to his car and left for his destination, feeling amused at Sergeant Halstead's request.

Chapter 21

At the offices of Trent, Randolph, and Lambert, Melanie walked in and was confronted by her husband's secretary. "Hello, Mrs. Lambert, nice to see you again. Mr. Lambert is at a meeting in the conference room, but he should be out shortly."

"I'll wait in his office, Brenda," replied Melanie. "I'll surprise him as he walks in."

"All right, Mrs. Lambert, I won't warn him that you are here."

Melanie sat down in the leather chair that was behind Alan's desk. Being in good spirits and feeling almost childlike, she swung from side to side then turned around to face the window. She admired the view for a while until she heard the door open. Melanie turned back to face the desk.

Alan's secretary, Brenda, walked in, carrying something in her hand. "Here's the afternoon mail." She placed the mail on Alan's desk and then looked up at Melanie. "Would you care for some coffee or a magazine to read while you wait?"

"Oh no, thank you. I'll find something to do to pass the time."

"I'm sure it won't be too long before Mr. Lambert returns." Brenda smiled at Melanie and left the room.

Melanie observed the stack of mail before her and then began flipping through it. She recognized a few of the names that Alan would occasionally mention. She saw one from Stone Pharmaceutical Labs and the last one from the New England Cancer Institute. Alan never mentioned having a client from there, she thought. She wondered who it could be and why this person contacted her husband. In the lefthand corner, it was marked Personal. My, how mysterious, she thought.

Melanie then began looking about her husband's desk, shuffling things around a bit. *Doesn't he have a letter opener?* she wondered. *If I don't find it, I will have to buy him one, one that is very special. How much longer will I have to wait? His meeting is lasting a long time.* Melanie was feeling rather bored and rather listless. She turned to his computer and clicked it on. She saw a list of e-mails and looked through the list. She noticed one from Dr. Dan Ulrich. She clicked on to it and read a short note telling Alan that he had received something in the mail. That made her even more curious. Melanie then clicked on to the sent mail. There was one for Dr. Dan Ulrich. *Is Alan sick but has not said anything to me? I need to know if he is sick.* Her curiosity had to be satisfied. She opened it and began to read.

At first, Melanie felt confused, but as she continued reading, she realized that these were the threat notes that had been sent to her father while he was in the hospital. What on earth was Alan doing with the threat notes? Why had he sent them to Dr. Ulrich, and what was this all about?

As she sat in deep contemplation, she suddenly heard her husband's voice. "Melanie, what are you doing here? What do you have there? Have you been looking through my e-mails?" Alan questioned with a sharp edge to his voice.

"I was bored, so I started looking through the computer files. I was also looking for a letter opener but didn't find one."

"So you were going to open my mail as well!" Alan was growing more irascible by the minute.

"No, Alan, will you let me explain? I was merely wondering whether you had a letter opener. If I wasn't able to find one, I was going to buy one for you. Besides, what difference does it make? After all, I am your wife. We shouldn't have any secrets from each other."

"The business I have with my clients has to be confidential. It would be extremely unethical to discuss them with anyone, including you. I thought you understood that, Melanie."

She felt her anger surfacing as he spoke. He had never before lived up to that profound statement. But that was beside the point. Her primary interest was in the threat notes she found in his e-mail. "I think there is more involved here than just the confidentiality to your clients," Melanie replied. "I found the threat notes in your e-mail. You had sent them to Dr. Dan Ulrich. At first, I thought that you were ill when I saw communication with the cancer institute. But further investigation revealed something entirely different. Would you explain this to me, Alan?" Melanie was beginning to tremble, wondering what her husband would reveal. "I don't know what to think. You have been unusually short-tempered lately, as if something has been bothering you."

"Why didn't you warn me that you were stopping by my office, Melanie?"

"I was shopping in town and thought I would surprise you, possibly even go to lunch together."

"Well, you certainly did surprise me, and as for lunch, I'm afraid I couldn't eat a thing."

"What is wrong, Alan?" Melanie asked, feeling a great deal of consternation enveloping her. "What are you doing with the threat notes, and why did you send them to Dr. Ulrich?"

"I had them in my possession, and I sent them to him."

"Why would you send them to Dr. Ulrich? Why would he have an interest in them?"

"All right, Melanie, since you're so curious, I am the one who authored the threat notes," Alan replied.

"Oh no, Alan, why would you do that? How could you?" Fear and disbelief were running cold through her veins.

"It was nothing but a scare tactic so that Stone Labs would not begin to manufacture and distribute the anticancer agent that Ivan had developed. They were empty threats, nothing more."

Melanie stared at her husband, and her face became a study of bewilderment. "You knew about the formula all along. I think maybe you'd better tell me everything, Alan. I have to know."

"Well, I don't know where to begin, except that everything was supposed to be clean and simple, but things got out of hand. Shortly after your father was admitted to the hospital, I was approached by

Dr. Ulrich, who is on staff at the New England Cancer Institute. I had been visiting with your father, clearing up some legal matters, when Dr. Ulrich stopped me in the hall. He said that he remembered me from years ago, when Trent had defended him in a malpractice lawsuit. I did all the research and accompanied him at the trial as second chair. He had reminded me of the case where the parents of a young girl were suing him. Do you remember, I told you about this case? They claimed that he had performed more radical surgery than was necessary on their daughter's jaw, which was afflicted with a malignancy. As a result, the girl was disfigured. She apparently had reconstructive surgery done, and her parents wanted to recoup the money for the surgery. The judge sided with the young girl, and Ulrich was practically ruined. It took him a very long time to regain himself and his career following the trial."

Melanie listened to Alan searchingly. "Yes, I do remember that very sad story. What does it have to do with the threat notes and the formula?"

Alan continued. "I had an appointment with Ulrich a few days later at his office, and he talked at length about the malpractice case. Apparently, the girl had been a model and was very quickly rising to the top when the malignant growth had been discovered. Because of the suit, Ulrich had gained much notoriety, and it had a very detrimental effect on him and his career.

"He knew that your father was in the hospital and suffering from Leukemia. Ulrich had been experimenting on a drug which was proving to be very successful, especially in Leukemia patients. He wanted to enter your father onto the study he was conducting. He wanted me to try to convince your father that I owed him that much. He felt that if he could cure someone as prominent as your father and be the first with a cure, it would prove to be very prestigious as well as rewarding for him. It would help his career immensely, of course.

"Since I handled all important documents for the Stone Labs, I had come upon something that suggested to me that there was some sort of secret formula in existence about which no one knew. It could have been anything, but I suspected it might be for something long sought after, like cancer. I reiterated this to Dan Ulrich. Well, when he heard that, he practically went wild. For a moment, I thought he was going to become violent."

Melanie was feeling very anxious with dread of what more information there was to come.

Alan then continued. "He said that he wanted me to find out about the secret formula if there existed one and that he would pay me well for the information. He wanted to tap your father's phone and anyone else's who might know about it. As it turned out, there actually was a secret formula, and Ivan was the only other person who knew about it. We eventually found that out through a conversation he and Mac had over the phone. Ivan tried to get your father to take the new wonder drug Ivan had developed and save his own life. It was far superior to Ulrich's drug, which had only a 70 percent success rate and still rather toxic as opposed to a 99 percent success rate with Ivan's drug with no toxicity. Surprisingly, because of the threat notes being sent, he refused. We made him believe that Marissa was in danger, and as you know, he feared for her safety, as well as for the other members of the family. Please know that I would never allow anything to happen to Marissa."

"Did you plant the bugging devices, Alan?" Melanie asked in horror.

"No, I didn't have to. Ulrich found someone who works in the maintenance department of the hospital to do that. He took care of bugging the phones."

"Which phones had been bugged?" Melanie asked.

"Only your dad's hospital phone and Ivan's home phone were tapped."

"I can't imagine anyone agreeing to something like this. Why would they?"

"Well, Ulrich promised him a supervisory position in the maintenance department at the cancer institute and also paid him off well. Ulrich was able to obtain grants for his research due to the nature of it and the fact that he has been very successful in curing many of his patients. The maintenance guy was also asked to stalk Marissa and to get to know her habits so that she could be placed in a vulnerable position in case she had to be used as a wedge. I assure you that they were empty threats. She would not be harmed."

"Does this person have a chipped front tooth by some remote chance, and is he middle-aged?" Melanie questioned. "Marissa described him very well."

"Why, yes, Marissa is very observant," Alan acknowledged.

Melanie rose from her chair and began to pace. She stopped as she reached the window and stared out at the same view she saw less than an hour ago, but now, it looked tarnished with the close scrutiny of reality. "I feel as if I've been living my life in a semicomatose state. All of this was going on right under my nose, and I didn't realize it." She turned to face her husband, who had his head down toward the floor and glanced up as she spoke. "I feel as if I were seeing you for the first time, Alan. I don't seem to know you at all. After all these years, I didn't know that you were capable of so much deception." Desperately holding back the tears, Melanie's voice began to tremble. "What I simply cannot understand is why you agreed to do this for Dr. Ulrich."

"I felt that I owed it to him. I felt partially responsible for him losing the case. Besides, it was a terrific offer monetarily."

"But we don't need the money," Melanie said, feeling exasperated. "Becoming the legal counsel for Stone Labs was a wonderful opportunity for you. And you have the partnership in a prominent law firm. What more did you want?"

Alan walked over to where Melanie was standing and held her by the shoulders. "Don't you see that everything I have I owe to Stone Labs? I'm a product of your father's company. Your family has a patent on me. Melanie, I need to do something on my own. I know that this wasn't the way to do it, but Ulrich wasn't really asking for very much, so I complied with his plan. After all, I felt bad for the guy when we lost the case. I was the one who blew it for him. Trent didn't have time to do any research. He was on another important case at the time, so he let me take over most of it. But he did accept the responsibility for losing it. So you can imagine how I felt."

Melanie looked into her husband's eyes, wondering if she could ever believe in him again. "I just don't know, Alan. You turned against the one person who did the most for you. He paid for his kindness with his life."

"That's not true, and you know it! He could have taken his wonder drug himself, but he chose not to. He even refused the opportunity that Ulrich gave him of being placed on his study. He refused that too! It was his way of dying as a hero. He wanted to die, Melanie."

"Someone with so much to live for would not want to die. You know why he did it. You were there at the reading of the will and his letter. He was protecting his family. He also felt he owed it as retribution for the lives his drug could have saved. You and Dr. Ulrich stopped him from manufacturing it. And what about Ivan—he lost his life because of your chicanery. He wouldn't have been out on that stormy night if all of this hadn't happened. Both he and Greg felt the formula would be safer with Greg. As you know, someone had broken into Ivan's lab and his home."

"Yes, I know. It was Joe Slater from the hospital maintenance department. He was looking for the formula at the time but had no success. Ulrich thought that if he got the formula, that would be the end of the entire mess. But that plan didn't work out."

"Alan, what do you know about Ivan's death? Was that planned too? The paper said something about another set of tire tracks going across the road which appeared rather suspicious."

"I don't know anything about that, Melanie, I swear. Ivan's death was an accident. That is all I know. You don't think I'm capable of murder, do you?"

Melanie's eyes flashed at him. "Oh my God, I hope you're not!"

Chapter 22

The evening had arrived quickly. The sun seemed rushed to hide beneath the horizon, and darkness overtook the daylight.

The phone rang at the Stone residence. Greg threw the newspaper to the floor and hurried to answer it.

"Hello, Mr. Stone, this is Sergeant Halstead. How are you this evening?"

"Just fine," Greg replied. "Do you have anything for me?"

"Yes, as a matter of fact. I checked on the license number you gave me. The truck is registered to a Joe Slater. You gave me enough to bring him in for questioning. We will see what we can find out from him."

"Who is this Joe Slater?" Greg inquired.

"He works in the maintenance department at the hospital. Also, according to Marissa's description of her stalker, this is our guy. We will check out his vehicle and see if that metal strip you found at the accident scene definitely belongs to his truck."

"Sounds good, Sergeant Halstead. What about the wiretaps? Have you checked them out? Apparently, my dad's and Ivan's phone calls were being monitored. Someone was after the formula that Ivan had developed and found the opportunity to destroy it along with Ivan as well."

"This is a rather involved case. We did not get any fingerprints from Ivan's phone but did get some from your father's phone. If they belong to Joe Slater, they can be easily explained away because he maintains the phones at the hospital."

"Thank you for the information, Sergeant Halstead. Keep in touch in case you get any more information."

"Okay, I certainly will do that. Good-bye for now, and don't worry, Mr. Stone, we will get to the bottom of this case very soon."

As Greg walked away from the phone, he heard Vanessa's voice. She and their daughter, Marissa, came into the living room. "To whom were you speaking on the phone?" Vanessa inquired.

"It was Sergeant Halstead, and he told me some information he had on the case. As you know, there were tire tracks going across the road in the direction of the point where Ivan's car went down the cliff. I found a piece of metal stripping at the site, which matched the trim on a truck that turned out to belong to someone who works at the hospital. I also noticed that there were brown scratches on the truck matching that of Ivan's car."

"When did you do all of this?" asked Vanessa.

"I was at the hospital today," Greg continued. He told her about seeing the truck with the brown scratches on it and also the missing piece of metal trim. He described about the bugging devices and how the police had checked for fingerprints to find out who inserted the microphones. He also related how he gave the license plate number of the truck to be checked by the police to find out who was the owner. "The truck is owned by a Joe Slater, as it turns out, who matches the description you gave of your stalker, Marissa. Sergeant Halstead has arrested him and will be questioning him."

"Well, that kind of news is a relief," Marissa replied.

Greg stared at his daughter for a moment. "Now that the formula is gone along with the scientist who discovered it, there is no reason for you, Marissa, to be in any danger."

Greg then decided to change the conversation at this point and pretended to assume a feeling of complacency. Just as he was about to speak, the doorbell rang, creating a distraction. He opened the door to see Paul Glasser standing at the entrance.

"Hello, Mr. Stone, is Marissa ready to go?"

"To go where?" asked Greg.

"Didn't Marissa tell you? We're going to see a movie."

"No, Paul, she didn't, but then, I didn't give her much opportunity to do that. I'm afraid that I monopolized the conversation this evening."

"Just then, Marissa came walking into the foyer, where the two men stood. She kissed her father on the cheek and bid him good-bye. "We won't be very late. See you later, Dad. We'll be gone for only a couple of hours."

The young couple closed the door behind them, and Greg went back to the living room to where his wife sat. She looked up at Greg as he walked in. "Looks like we have the evening to ourselves," Vanessa announced.

"Yes, it should be a quiet evening at that," replied Greg.

* * *

A crowd of people walked out of the movie theater, dispersing in various directions, some progressing toward the large parking lot. In the midst of the crowd, Marissa and Paul walked hand in hand and discussed the mysterious plot of the movie they had just seen. As they approached Paul's car, he asked, "What would you like to do now? How about going to my place for a while, where we can spend some time alone? Would you like that, Marissa?" They reached the car, and he opened the door for her, waiting for her answer.

Marissa quickly slipped into the passenger seat and waited till he was seated beside her. "I can't be with you that way, Paul, at least not just yet."

Paul felt a flash of some annoyance run through him. "Marissa, we have been dating for several weeks now. When will you be ready?"

"I don't know, Paul. I don't expect you to understand, but I need more time. It's important for me to be emotionally ready first, and I don't feel that I am. I am sorry, Paul."

Paul had his arm around her and began kissing the side of her face and down her neck. "Baby, I love you. I need you so much."

Marissa felt herself weakening. She liked him. That was a start of building a relationship, but she needed stronger feelings to make any kind of commitment. She was very quiet as they drove, and before she realized where they were, Paul pulled up to his apartment.

"Just come in for a little while, Marissa. I have a surprise for you. Come, let's go in."

Paul took her hand, and they walked up the stairs to the front door, and after he unlocked it, they went inside. "Have a seat on the sofa, and I will fix us drinks. You will love it." Paul busied himself at the bar, where he had all of the supplies that he needed.

Marissa amused herself with a magazine in anticipation of the special drink that she was promised. "Don't make the drink too strong, Paul. You know I'm not used to drinking."

Paul returned carrying two glasses filled to the top with a creamy and frothy beverage. "There you are, my love. It's a pineapple-and-coconut drink mixed with a little rum."

Marissa took a small taste to sample it. "Hmm, you were right, I do like it. Now what is the surprise you have for me?"

"Have a few more sips of your drink, and I'll get it."

The drink went down smoothly. Marissa felt very thirsty, so she drank half of the drink by the time Paul returned. She was beginning to feel slightly light-headed.

"That drink certainly must agree with you, Marissa. When you're done, I have more in the pitcher up on the bar if you want."

"No, I'll pass. I must be drinking it too quickly. My head is beginning to spin."

"Just relax and sit back," Paul said soothingly as he put his arm around her. He then reached into his pocket and pulled out a ring and handed it to her. "This is the surprise I promised you."

The room began to move in strange directions, as if she were sitting on a large water bed. As Marissa looked at the ring, she had a slightly distorted view of what she was seeing. "This is my ruby ring," she acknowledged with a few decibels just short of shouting. "Where did you get my ring?"

"Someone at the hospital had it. He said that he works part-time at the restaurant where we had dinner that night, and he found it when he was cleaning up. He also works in the maintenance department at the hospital and had seen us there before."

"I thought someone had stolen it at the restaurant that evening." Marissa was feeling slightly more alert suddenly due to the shock of seeing her ring. "I thought that it fell into the hands of the person who was writing the threat notes. After all, the ring was mentioned in one of those notes. What a strange coincidence that you should have it." She then put the ring on her finger. "I'm so relieved to have it back. You can't imagine how upset I was to lose it."

"Oh yes, I can. I was with you when you lost it. Now finish your drink." He lifted the glass from the table and handed it to her.

Marissa held the glass in her hand. She hesitated a moment before drinking. Marissa finished her drink and placed the empty glass on the table. "That was a terrific drink, and now it's time to call it a night." She rose to her feet but felt a bit strange. "I shouldn't have had the drink, but I thought only one drink wouldn't bother me. I simply drank it too fast."

Paul gently pulled her back on the sofa and embraced her. He then kissed her long and fervently, hoping to arouse her.

Marissa tried to summon all of her strength to pull away from him but felt very weak and helpless. She felt light-headed, and Paul's voice no longer seemed to be coming from him but echoed from across the room. She tried desperately to free herself, but it was to no avail. "I think there was more in that drink than rum," she said. "Paul, wait, I have to ask you something. Did you know the man who took my ring at the restaurant?"

"Yes, my love, I did," he said derisively. "I was involved in a little plan which paid off very well and will continue to pay off for quite some time. The best part of it was that I got to meet you. All I had to do was get something of yours that you valued, and so I did. By simply doing that, I was promised a position at the cancer institute, which seemed like a good deal. Joe Slater came up to me at the hospital and returned the ring. I was relieved that he did what he was supposed to do."

"So this Joe Slater was part of the plan to frighten me?"

"Yes, apparently so, but he didn't hurt you."

"No, but was he the one who was stalking me as well? Some middle-aged man seemed to be everywhere that I went and seemed to be watching and following me. He even asked me for directions at one point. That was scary. What was it all about?"

"Just sit back and relax. It's all over with," Paul said, trying to calm her. "I put a mild hallucinogen in the drink to relax you. In a moment, you will feel like you're floating on air." He placed her head on his shoulder and put his arm around her again.

Marissa heard soothing music in the background and began to fall asleep. She felt herself being carried to another room and then being placed on a bed. Her clothes and her shoes were being removed. She also felt Paul placing a throw on her, and it felt warm and comforting. She felt him place his mouth on hers, pressing against it. Marissa felt very weak and helpless. Her head was swimming, and everything in the room was becoming distorted. She tried desperately to free herself but did not have the strength. She felt Paul's hands caressing her entire body. She felt her body respond and then fell into a deep sleep.

A few hours had passed when Marissa awoke. Paul was asleep next to her, letting out an occasional snore. The memory of the previous evening seemed hazy and rather nebulous. She found herself completely undressed. The events came back to her in small doses, but she had no recollection of consenting to sleep with Paul. How long had she been here? How did she get herself into this predicament? The digital clock on the nightstand had just flipped to 2:00 a.m. A feeling of fear crept into her, but she had no memory of why she was frightened. All she knew was that she must get home. There were things that Paul had confided to her last night that were rather puzzling. Why did Paul have her ring and have given it to this person who was stalking her, and why did he say that he was promised a position at the cancer institute? He was simply using her. It did not make sense. *He doesn't really love me. He is lying, and I don't want anything more to do with him.*

Carefully, she got up out of bed and stumbled over her shoes that had been on the floor near the bed. She put them on and looked for her clothes and quickly put them on. She then looked for her purse. For a moment, she heard Paul making stirring noises. She quickly pulled out her cell phone and called a cab. After putting the phone back in her purse, she wondered whether her wallet held enough money to pay for the cab. Trembling, she fumbled through her purse. Finding her wallet,

Marissa searched through it and found enough money to get her home. Relieved, she went into the living room and sat back in a chair by the window. Silently, she began her vigil till the cab would come into view outside the apartment.

There were two glasses on the cocktail table, and she did recall having a drink. That drink had more than rum in it, something she had not expected. The rushing and the anticipation of getting home were giving her a headache that was building into somewhat of a crescendo. She couldn't wait till she was back safely at home and able to lie down peacefully in her own bed.

As she looked down at her hands, she saw the beautiful ruby ring back on her finger. Paul's story about the ring seemed rather implausible. She would have to make him explain more fully about what he had gotten himself involved in. He did mention something about a plan. Suddenly, she heard her name from across the room.

"Marissa, what are you doing?" Paul was coming over to where she was sitting by the window. His hair was all disheveled, and he had a strange expression on his face.

"I couldn't sleep, Paul. I have a very bad headache, and I would like to go home. What did you put in my drink to make me so drowsy?"

Paul glanced at the clock. "It's after two o'clock. You need to get back into bed and get some restful sleep. I just put something a little calming into your drink so that it would relax you."

At that moment, she noticed the headlights of a cab as it pulled up outside. The horn blew almost as soon as the cab stopped outside the apartment. Paul looked toward the window. "Who's blowing the horn at this time?" His brow was knitted in bewilderment as he advanced in the direction of the window to where Marissa sat. "There is a cab down there. Who's going out at this time of night?"

Marissa got up from the chair. "I am, Paul. I'm going home."

"No, Marissa, I don't want you to leave like this. Now, be a good girl and come back to bed." He grabbed at her arm and began leading her back toward the bedroom.

Outside, the horn blew again, and Marissa pulled away from him. "I have to leave, Paul. I have to leave now." She went to the door and opened it. She ran out and slammed it behind her. Practically stumbling down the stairs, she finally reached the bottom and was out the main entrance to the street. The cab was about to pull away. Just then, she quickly hailed it back. In a moment, she was seated inside the cab and was off, leaving Paul upstairs, watching out the window.

Oh hell, I thought she would be more compliant this morning. I will have to see her again, maybe just one more time, Paul thought. *She was a cute little thing but a little naïve. I planned to have a little more fun with her, but I have a feeling she remembered more than I thought she would.* He lingered at the window, watching the cab as it made its way down the street.

Chapter 23

Greg and Vanessa sat at the breakfast table and had their second cup of coffee. Greg looked up from the newspaper. "So is everything all set for tonight's dinner party? What fabulous entrée is on the menu?"

"We're having veal oscar tonight," Van replied. "Nora is going to help serve and also help with all of the other preparations as well. She will be here in about an hour."

"She's been quite a find, hasn't she? How long has Nora been in our service?" Greg looked at Vanessa questioningly.

"Oh, I guess it has been about seven years now. She has been wonderful for our dinner parties. I don't know what I'd do without her. Life would be a little more difficult if we hadn't found her."

"Say, did you notice what time our daughter strolled in this morning?"

"No, Greg, I didn't, but it must have been very late. I woke up for only a moment when I heard her on the stairs, but then, I went right back to sleep."

"It was about two forty-five," replied Greg. "I wasn't able to sleep very well until Marissa did finally get home. When they were leaving for the movie, Marissa did say that they wouldn't be late. Besides that, I've got a funny feeling about Paul. I don't completely trust him. There is something about him. I can't quite put my finger on it just yet. Naturally, I was worried. Marissa doesn't normally stay out that late either."

"You certainly are a suspicious one, Greg. But I will agree that it was very late for Marissa to be coming home. Wonder what she will have to say for herself."

* * *

It was late in the morning when Marissa awoke with a start. She bolted upright into a sitting position and cried out, "No, Paul, leave me alone, leave me alone!" Marissa looked around the room and realized that she was safely home in her own bed. The events of the previous evening were all coming back to her. She looked at her ring again and remembered Paul telling her that he did know the man who was stalking her and had her ring.

Just then, Greg was coming upstairs and overheard Marissa's cries. He opened her door and saw, to his dismay, a very distressed Marissa sitting on her bed, fully clothed in the same outfit she had worn on her date last night.

"Honey, what's wrong?" Greg asked as he walked over to her. He tried to comfort his daughter. "Marissa, tell me what are you talking about? You came in very late. I was terribly worried about you."

Marissa managed to finally gain control of herself and was able to answer. "I was talking about Paul. I think the reason he dated me was because it helped him get a position at the cancer institute that he was promised. Paul said that he was involved in a little scheme or conspiracy and needed to get my birthstone ring. He gave it back to me last evening. He said all he had to do was give the ring to someone at the hospital and that he would get it back, and he did. I don't know what to think about him. He gave me a drink and put something in it that made me feel relaxed. It made me drowsy enough that I fell asleep. While I was falling asleep, he took advantage of me. When I awoke, I decided to go home as soon as possible, and so I called a cab. He tried to stop me, but I wouldn't listen to him. I really don't trust him anymore."

Greg just held Marissa in his arms, trying to soothe her. "What kind of conspiracy was he involved in that he needed to get your ring?" Greg tried desperately to contain his anger, which was now ready to erupt like a fulminating volcano. The threat of his daughter being victimized had been fulfilled even after he thought the danger was over. Paul had been a part of this dreadful plot, just as he had suspected. Damn him, he thought, for taking advantage of a sweet and vulnerable girl like his daughter. And his father and Ivan as well were used in a dangerous and evil scheme that cost them their lives. "This is just too much," Greg said aloud. "I can't believe that this is all happening. We will get to the bottom of it soon, I promise you, Marissa."

Marissa stopped crying and looked up at her father. "I hope so, Dad. All along, I thought that Paul cared for me, even more so than I cared for him. How could I have been so foolish? He was putting on this phony façade for my benefit, and I believed him. The one thing I didn't like about him though was that he became very controlling. It was almost too pronounced. We always seemed to do things his way, as if I had no say in the matter. Lately, he rarely consulted with me about our plans. He simply called and told me how we were going to spend any particular evening. Last evening, I didn't want to go to his apartment, but he wouldn't listen to my request. He just simply drove there. Many times, he said that he'd do anything to get ahead. I guess that included me as well."

"Guess he was far too enterprising for his own good. Using people in this way is not the way to get ahead. He could end up in a lot of trouble and could cost him more than he had bargained for." Greg stood up and began to walk out of Marissa's room. "Come on down, honey, and get some breakfast. Your mother is preparing for tonight's dinner party, and she hopes you will join us. Do you think you'll be up for it?"

"I don't know, Dad. I'll wait on that decision after I've had some coffee. See you downstairs."

Greg went down to the kitchen, where Vanessa was busying herself with preparations for the dinner. Nora had arrived and was in the dining room, attending to the table linens and the dinnerware that would be used that evening. Greg told his wife everything that had transpired when he spoke to Marissa.

Vanessa looked with shock and horror at what she had heard. "How could I have been so wrong about Paul? He was always very polite, and I was also impressed by the fact that he was such an aspiring young doctor. Poor Marissa. I really feel bad for her."

Greg put his arms on his wife's shoulders. "Don't worry. Marissa will be just fine. Richard Brooks is going to be here this evening. He can check her to see how she is doing. I'm going to call Sergeant Halstead and tell him about last night's incident."

The phone rang in Sergeant Halstead's office, and he reached to answer it. "I'm glad you called, Mr. Stone," Sergeant Halstead acknowledged. "We have Joe Slater here now for questioning. It seems that he was with one of the nurses on the night Mr. Kerensky was killed in the accident. He seems to feel confident that he'll skate this thing since he seems to have an alibi. We're not completely satisfied though. The nurse will be in for questioning too. Don't worry, Mr. Stone, if Slater is guilty, he will pay for his crime."

"I'm relieved to hear that, Sergeant Halstead. Hope he gets what he deserves. I will be waiting to hear from you if you learn anything more." Greg then related the story that Marissa told him about the previous evening and how Paul admitted to being a part of a conspiracy and how he was able to get Marissa's ring.

"Well, that is interesting, Mr. Stone," Sergeant Halstead replied. "I will have to look into that as well and see how Paul Glasser is involved in this case. For now, just try to relax. It's in our hands now. I will keep you apprised of any developments when I have them."

The evening came quickly. All the preparations had been completed for the dinner, and Vanessa was upstairs, putting on the finishing touches to her outfit. She stood before a full-length mirror and saw a tall, slender woman with medium-length, warm-brown hair worn in a simple style. Vanessa looked very attractive in her teal blue silk dress. It emphasized her slim figure. She carefully chose her jewelry, which would be pearls. They would look well against the deep shade of her dress.

Downstairs, Greg heard the doorbell chime and went to greet the first arrival. "Hello, Mom, how are you this evening?"

"I'm just fine, son," Lenore answered as she handed Greg a package. "Here you are. I've brought you pastry that I fussed over this afternoon. I hope that you and your family enjoy it as much as I enjoyed making it."

"That was very thoughtful of you, Mom," Greg said as he kissed his mother's cheek.

"Speaking of your family, where are Vanessa and Marissa?"

"Here I am," answered Vanessa, as she descended the stairs. "You look well rested," she said to Lenore as she walked over to greet her with a kiss.

"Oh yes, Vanessa, I'm finally able to fall asleep at night. It has been a long time since I've been able to do that. But I still miss Mac so very much. Nothing will ever be the same without him."

"It was a dreadful ordeal for you, Mother," Greg acknowledged, "and for all of us." He ushered his mother into the living room, where they seated themselves beside the fireplace. Greg then took the pastry to the kitchen, where Nora was busy with the last-minute preparations for the dinner. "How is everything shaping up, Nora? Will we be eating soon? Everything smells great. My mother brought some pastry which you may serve later."

Nora took the pastry from Greg and placed it on the counter in the butler's pantry. "This looks very delicious. I must get the recipe from your mother. And, Mr. Stone, I will be serving dinner very shortly, soon after the last guest arrives."

Greg returned to the living room, where Dr. Richard Brooks had joined the others, and Marissa had also come downstairs.

"There's the old man," Dr. Brooks chided. "Were you helping Nora with the dinner in the kitchen? You know what they say about too many cooks spoiling the broth."

"Never mind the cynical humor, Richard. Wait till you taste the dinner. We are having veal oscar, which happens to be the specialty of this house."

"Now that is definitely a gourmet dish. It's one I had in one of those restaurants at Quincy Market and loved it. But I'm sure it can't come close to this one, especially if Vanessa had anything to do with it." Dr. Brooks smiled and glanced at Vanessa.

She returned his smile and thanked him for his compliment. "It is my recipe, but Nora did help me with it. She is wonderful. We are very grateful to have her."

At that moment, the doorbell chimed again, interrupting the conversation. Nora quickly went to answer it.

"Hello, Nora, it's good to see you again."

"Hello, Mrs. Lambert, it's a pleasure to see you too. Everyone is in the living room, waiting for you."

Melanie walked into the living room and greeted everyone. She showed evidence of some strain and nervousness that was not at all like the typical Melanie the family had always known.

"Isn't Alan going to join us this evening, Melanie?" Greg asked. "It's not his work that is keeping him away tonight, is it?"

"Oh no," Melanie answered, "he simply didn't feel well and gives everyone his regrets."

"And where are Mark and Derek?" Lenore inquired from across the room. "I was so looking forward to seeing them this evening."

"The boys are spending this weekend at Boy Scout camp. I'm very sorry that they had to miss a family dinner, but this campout has been planned for quite some time. You will be seeing them very soon, I promise."

* * *

Dr. Ulrich sat at his desk at home and was contemplating what had happened. He wondered how his plan was progressing but worried that there would be some slipup. He felt that he had gotten too many people involved. It was all a rather precarious balance and that it would take only one slip of the tongue and all would be lost. He made several promises that he wasn't sure he would keep, especially to that maintenance worker. He was going to be the fall guy who would take all the blame. Eventually, he would be out of the picture, and he wouldn't have to be concerned about him.

I need to get some publicity regarding my chemo medication so that I can get a grant for more research. I need the money. Too bad I couldn't convince Mac Stone to take the medication, and he would probably have gone into remission. He was such a stubborn man. I should have been more persistent with him. Oh well, his formula is gone now, and I won't have his competition to contend with. I will be first with my formula. Victory will be mine!

He turned to his computer and began to write his proposal for a grant, which he felt would not be too difficult to acquire.

Chapter 24

The dinner bell rang, and everyone filed into the dining room to be seated at the long and elegantly appointed table. Two silver candelabras stood regally at either end. A glittering crystal chandelier hung in the center of the room over the table. Dinner was brought in, and Nora served it with a flourish that only came with years of experience. It was acknowledged by the guests that the dinner was done to perfection.

Lenore observed Melanie, who sat across from her. She could not help but notice that her daughter appeared to be tired and somewhat withdrawn from the conversation. "Melanie, dear, are you feeling well tonight? You don't seem to be in very good spirits. I do wish that Alan could have been here."

"I'm fine, Mom, really. Maybe just a little tired, that's all. It's nothing to worry about."

Melanie could not bring herself to tell her mother that Alan was involved in the conspiracy that brought about her father's death and that he was the one who authored the threat notes. Her pride would not allow it. It was difficult for her to believe that Alan had actually admitted to being guilty of these dreadful crimes. He even sold out the company that hired him, her father's company, where he was given a wonderful career opportunity. He became like Judas, selling out her father for a few pieces of silver—money that they did not need. She could not fully comprehend the motives as being essential enough to have done so much harm.

Greg, overhearing the conversation between his mother and sister, was wondering what exactly was troubling Melanie. The fact that Alan hadn't shown up also troubled him. He was not a man who was prone to illness, and he never before missed a family gathering. He thought that later, if he had an opportunity, he would quietly broach the subject with his sister. He also hoped that Sergeant Halstead would uncover more evidence in the conspiracy and that he would hear from him again very soon. The suspense was unnerving. Paul certainly was not the only one involved. He had nothing to gain simply on his own. There had to be more to it.

The conversation had proceeded on to more jovial topics. Vanessa discussed her interest in golf. She had played in several tournaments and was rather good at the game.

"It has been quite challenging but also a lot of fun. I really love the game."

Marissa was a sophomore at Boston College and had many interesting stories to tell about school. She also mentioned the courses she was taking in business management. Her intent was to join the Stone Pharmaceutical Company after graduation, hopefully, in an administrative capacity. She had the ability for organization and the business sense of both her father and grandfather.

"I look forward to someday carry on in the family tradition of taking over as president of the company. It was a dream which I have held on to and intend to fulfill," Marissa said. "I want to be the first woman to run the company, and I intend to prove that I am very capable and intelligent enough for the position." She was determined that no man would ever push her around again and force her into a situation that was not of her intent.

Lenore then spoke. "Well, that is quite an ambitious endeavor, Marissa. I wish you the very best and hope you succeed. I am sure that you will. I too have been thinking about my part in all of this with Mac gone. I have been learning all about the business. Mac had stipulated in his will that I be placed on the board of directors. Of course, I have been taking this request very seriously. Certainly, I will do my best for Mac and would never want to disappoint him, even now. He has sacrificed so much for this company."

Greg listened intently to his mother sounding as ambitious as his daughter about taking an active role in the company. He felt proud and elated. "Mother, one day this week, you must come down to the lab and be formally invested onto the board of directors. You seem very eager to get started with your new career."

"I am very eager," Lenore replied. "I try not to spend too much time at home alone. The house seems larger than ever now. Even though I have kept the housekeeper, I still get lonely."

"Why don't you sell the house and move into a town house on Beacon Hill?" Richard Brooks suggested. "I could find out if there is one available that would be suitable for you. I find that it suits my purposes just fine. For one person living alone, I find that a town house is the perfect solution."

"Well, I'm not so sure that I'm ready to give up the home that Mac and I shared all of these years. There are too many memories enshrined in it for me to simply let it go. It's a beautiful house, and I would like to keep it in the family. Someday, one of my grandchildren may want to live in it with their family, should they decide to marry. Perhaps Marissa or one of your twins, Melanie, will make it their home."

Melanie smiled at her mother. "The twins are rather young as yet. It will be quite some time before either one of them marries. I suspect it'll take them a long time to mature."

Lenore looked over to Marissa. "Marissa is growing up very quickly and, as I recall, is dating a fine doctor. For all we know, they may be making marriage plans already."

"Oh no, Grandmother, there is no chance of that. I don't ever intend to marry Paul Glasser." Marissa disliked being linked with Paul in any way, especially marriage. He had finally disappointed her completely.

Lenore looked at her granddaughter with bewilderment at the statement she had just heard. As she studied Marissa for a moment, the glimmer of the ruby ring on her finger caught the light and flashed in Lenore's eyes. "The ring, Marissa, you are wearing your ruby ring. When did you get it back?"

Marissa suddenly had a morose expression on her face. "Last night. Paul gave it to me. You see, Grandmother, it is a complicated story."

Lenore's face was a study of incomprehension. "I don't understand, Marissa. I was under the impression that some dreadful conspirator had stolen the ring from you. The ring was mentioned in the threat notes."

"Yes, that is all true, Grandmother."

The conversation was abruptly interrupted by the sound of the ringing telephone. Nora quickly left the kitchen to answer it.

"I wonder who that could be," Greg said. "Why don't we all go into the living room. Nora will serve coffee and dessert to us there, where it is more comfortable. If anyone would like an after-dinner brandy, feel free to help yourself at the bar."

As everyone retired into the living room, Nora walked in and over to Greg. She told him in a low voice, "Sergeant Halstead is on the phone and wants to speak with you, Mr. Stone."

"Thank you, Nora. I'll take it in the study." Greg walked out of the living room, across the foyer, and into the study. "Hello, Sergeant Halstead," Greg said as he lifted the handset to his ear. "You certainly have a long workday."

"I'm calling from my home. It occurred to me that you might want to know what I have as soon as possible rather than waiting for the news till after the weekend. Hope I didn't catch you at a bad time."

"No, on the contrary, you have perfect timing. We just finished eating dinner and were leaving the table when you called. Now, what is the news you have that couldn't wait till Monday? It must be something very important."

"I think you will find that it is, primarily because it hits close to home. As you know, we've questioned Joe Slater at length and the nurse who was with him, supposedly giving him an alibi the night Ivan Kerensky was killed. While questioning her for quite some time, we suspected that she was hiding something, and we were able to convince her that, if she was, she could get herself into a lot of trouble."

"Fearing this possibility, she confessed that the two of them went for a drive down the road in the direction of your home that night after Slater received a mysterious phone call. He refused to explain anything to the nurse. She said that they stopped and waited a short distance from the cliff area where Mr. Kerensky's car went over. As he saw the car approaching, he sped toward it. When he got closer, he said that this was the car he wanted and crossed over the centerline in the road directly toward Mr. Kerensky's car. He applied the brakes as he approached the other car, skidding and scraping against it. The other car careened over the edge and went down, bursting into flames at the bottom.

"The nurse said that she screamed at Slater, wanting to get out and help the victim, but he simply told her to shut up and never to breathe a word of it to anyone or she'd be sorry. When we finally got all the information out of her, she was trembling like crazy. So we let her go home, but Slater was kept for further interrogation."

Feeling the tremendous anger building up in him again, Greg blurted out, "Damn him, damn him to hell!"

"There is much more, Mr. Stone. After a few hours of interrogation and much convincing that Slater would get a lighter sentence if he confessed, Slater finally broke down and admitted all of it, including the phone taps. He also gave names of two others who were involved."

"Two others, Sergeant? Did you say he named two others?"

"Yes, that is correct, Mr. Stone. But I'm not at liberty to divulge their identity until they've been questioned."

"That's understandable, Sergeant Halstead. Thank you for calling with the information about Slater and the nurse. I sincerely appreciate it. And I'll be very eager to hear who were the other two involved whenever you're free to let me know their names."

"Right, Mr. Stone, I'll be in touch."

Greg hung up the phone and went back to the living room, where he had left all of his guests. He then walked over to the bar to fix himself a brandy.

Noticing some of Greg's agitation, Lenore spoke. "Greg, do you know what Marissa has just told us? Dr. Glasser was part of some kind of scheme or plan. She told us everything that he said to her last night. He may be surprised to hear that she remembered everything. Your poor child went through a great deal in the process."

"Yes, she certainly did," Greg admitted. "And I feel terribly responsible for allowing her to go out last night with that young man. As it was, I had my own suspicions about him but never let on to Marissa that I did. Thank God she returned home safely."

Vanessa nodded in agreement and put her emptied coffee cup on the table next to her. "What was that phone call all about?"

Greg seemed to weigh his words carefully as he spoke. "That was Sergeant Halstead. He told me that Joe Slater, from the hospital, was brought in for questioning along with a nurse who was out with him the night Ivan was killed." Greg continued with his interpretation of what Sergeant Halstead had told him on the phone. "Slater admitted that there were two others involved in this scheme, but Sergeant Halstead was not at liberty to give me their names until they were questioned."

"Two others!" Lenore exclaimed with dread and fear etching her face. "This is monstrous! I hope they all pay for their crimes against Mac and Ivan. I wonder who the other two could be. He didn't give you any clues?"

"No, he couldn't do that. I'd like to know who they are just as much as you do."

Vanessa sat next to Marissa and comforted her frightened and weeping daughter. "It's all right now, Marissa. No one will hurt you anymore. And whoever the other two are, they will be arrested very soon as well."

Marissa looked up at her mother. "One of them is probably that man who has been following me around with the dark glasses and chipped front tooth."

"I believe that was Joe Slater, honey," Greg interjected. "As far as I know, he has been the main character in this crime. It will be interesting to know the other two suspects."

Listening quietly to the conversation, Melanie became so agitated that she could not stop trembling. For she was the only one in the room who knew the ending to the story and the identity of the others involved.

"Looks like this case is really coming to a head," acknowledged Richard Brooks as he sipped a brandy. "It shouldn't be long before it's solved." He looked over at Greg, who was observing the nervous state in which his sister, Melanie, appeared. "Greg, do you have any ideas or any clues as to who the other two might be? You've been playing the part of the super sleuth lately. You've got to admit."

"Unfortunately, I don't have anything very concrete as yet. But, my dear Watson, only time will tell." Greg recalled one of his earlier conversations with Sergeant Halstead pertaining to the threat notes and who might have been the author.

"Melanie, are you feeling well?" Greg inquired as he kept noticing her agitation. "Is it possible that you might be coming down with whatever it is that has made Alan ill this evening?"

At the mention of Alan's name, Melanie became startled and almost wanted to cry. She needed to tell someone about what Alan had told her, but she simply could not do that. She felt too much loyalty toward him to do that. It was an impossible situation. She knew he was guilty of writing the threat notes, but she would never turn him in. Melanie loved her husband, but recently, she felt a strain in their relationship. Alan's own guilt was making him short-tempered and, at other times, very withdrawn. It had been difficult for Melanie to deal with so much inconsistency, and now this knowledge of his deeds was placed on her shoulders to bear alone and in confidence.

Suddenly, she heard her name called in a louder pitch than usual. "Melanie," Greg exclaimed, "I asked you if you were not feeling well."

"Oh, no, as a matter of fact, I'm not. I'm also worrying about Alan. Maybe it would be a good idea if I left. I'm sorry to break up the party, but I really must leave."

"Will you be well enough to drive yourself all the way home?" Vanessa asked with great concern.

"I'll take Melanie home," Dr. Brooks suggested. "You haven't looked well all evening, Melanie."

"I'll be just fine, really." Melanie tried to sound convincing; however, she was not.

"Now don't argue with the doctor, dear sister. He knows what's best." Greg looked very apprehensively at Melanie as he spoke. "We'll take care of your car and see that it gets back to you tomorrow."

Melanie finally relented and said her good-byes to everyone. She left with Richard Brooks, feeling tremendous relief from not having to face the family any longer. The evening had been painfully long for her, but now it was over, and she'd be able to relax again. She climbed into Richard's car, and they were on their way.

Richard glanced at Melanie, who was seated beside him.

"What is wrong with Alan this evening that he wasn't able to make the dinner?"

"Oh, he seems to be coming down with a cold or the flu. I don't really know except that he was not feeling well and felt I should go on to the dinner without him."

"If he's not asleep, would you like me to have a look at him? I could prescribe something that would make him feel better."

"That's very thoughtful of you, Richard, but he's probably asleep by now."

As they drove on, the conversation remained light and away from the topic of the conspiracy. Melanie was relieved not to have to make any more excuses. It was becoming exceedingly difficult to keep up appearances. She wasn't one to hold things in. In fact, she was just the opposite. Melanie had always been very open and honest. Those were her most admirable qualities, which she now had to cover up as if a curtain had been drawn.

Chapter 25

As they reached the home of Melanie and Alan Lambert, Richard pulled into the driveway, and Melanie alighted from the car. Richard followed her up the few steps to the front door. Melanie unlocked the door and walked inside.

"Thank you, Richard, for driving me home. It was so good of you to be concerned."

"Aren't you even going to ask me in? I'd really like to have a look at Alan, if I may. I'm a little worried about both of you."

"I'm sorry. That was rude of me to leave you standing outside. Come on in, although, like I said, Alan is probably asleep."

Richard walked in and closed the door behind him. He followed Melanie into the living room. It was a large room with enormous casement windows reaching from floor to the cathedral ceiling and to the loft above. The room was decorated in soft hues of camel and beige with accents of rust and cocoa brown.

"Melanie turned to face Richard. "Would you like something to drink?"

"No, thank you, Melanie. I had a brandy at Greg's house."

"Then I'll see if Alan is still awake." She left the room and searched the downstairs level for her husband, but he was nowhere to be found. *I was right*, she thought, *he must be asleep.*

Melanie climbed the stairs to where the bedrooms were situated. She looked in every room, but Alan was not there. Finally, she decided to check the loft, which Alan rarely used. Most of the time, however, this was her retreat, where she could spend a few quiet hours in solace doing the things she enjoyed, such as reading, sewing, or sometimes painting. She opened the door to the dark room. There she saw, silhouetted against the light coming from the living room downstairs, Alan's body hanging from the rafters near the railing. She choked back a scream, holding her hand against her mouth, and began to sob. "Alan, Alan, why did you do this?" She turned very pale and covered her face with her hands. It was too painful to find Alan in such a frightful way.

Hearing the sobbing noises, Richard quickly rushed upstairs, taking two steps at a time. As he reached the loft, he saw Melanie beginning to cry uncontrollably and looked up to see Alan's body hanging from the rafters. He rushed to check for a pulse, but there was none to be had. He determined that Alan had been dead for a couple of hours.

"Why would Alan do such a thing?" Richard took Melanie in his arms and tried to comfort her, but she would not stop her weeping. He cradled her gently in his arms, trying to soothe her, but the agony she had felt ever since Alan had confessed to her his part in the conspiracy was more than she could rationalize. Finding her husband dead was a hideous, climactic scene that brought all her emotions to the edge. She was no longer able to cope. She was dangerously close to a nervous collapse.

As Richard continued to soothe her, he noticed that there was a piece of paper on the table nearby. "Melanie, I think Alan left a note for you." He picked it up and handed it to Melanie. She read it out loud.

Dearest Melanie,

I can't face up to what I did or what I've done to you and the boys because of it. It is just a matter of time before I would be arrested for my transgressions. I have ruined our lives, and I know you would not want to be married to a criminal. Therefore, life without you would be impossible. I am very sorry that I have let you down. I felt this was my only option. Please forgive me.

With all my love,

Alan

"I should have seen it coming. Alan wasn't himself lately, but I never thought that he would resort to this," Melanie pensively said.

"What has he done that made him take his life?" asked Richard.

"He was the one who authored the threat notes. He did it for Dr. Ulrich because he felt he owed him. He helped represent him in a case that he had lost for him a long time ago." She related the entire story that Alan had revealed to her and why he felt he should fulfill this request for him. "Alan felt that Dr. Ulrich wasn't asking him to do very much, so he complied with his plan. He was also going to reward Alan monetarily. It was all part of a conspiracy that killed Uncle Ivan. Alan did tell me he had nothing to do with that."

Richard ushered Melanie out of the room and into her bedroom. "We will talk more about this later Melanie." Setting her down on the bed, he went to the loft and called the police. He then proceeded to call Greg, giving him the news of the latest tragedy.

Finally, after the police and the coroner arrived and questions were answered, the remains of Alan were taken from the loft. Richard then accompanied Melanie to the hospital along with her husband's body. "How could he have done all that he did and not have even given me a clue." Melanie felt that she would never get over all that had happened. "I wish that I had stayed home with Alan instead of making an appearance at the dinner party at Greg's home. I might then have prevented Alan, at least temporarily, from his suicide. In the end, I'm not so sure that I could have saved him from himself." She was hurting and believed that the worst betrayals come from those we love and trust the most.

When they reached the hospital, Melanie gave all of the pertinent information. It was late by then, so she would have to make arrangements for Alan's wake and burial in a couple of days. Melanie still felt tense and needed to reveal everything that she knew about the conspiracy.

"I've known everything for a couple days," Melanie confessed to Richard. "But I couldn't tell anyone. I discovered the threat notes on Alan's computer quite by accident. Otherwise, I may not have found out for a long time. I don't know how it all would have ended up."

"I understand how you must feel. If you hadn't discovered the threat notes, someone else might very well have found them on his computer. Since he didn't delete them, maybe somehow he must have wanted them to be discovered. It may have been a subconscious need."

They later left the hospital, and Richard returned Melanie back home. "Try to relax and maybe get some sleep. It is the best medicine for you now."

"I'm not sure that I can sleep. I am tired, but I don't think I can relax."

Richard put his arm around Melanie, and her head rested heavily against him. Occasionally, she would talk but then would become silent and finally dozed off. Richard laid her down across the sofa and covered her with an afghan that had been on an ottoman nearby. He sat in a chair across from her, admiring the softness of her features and the blond hair that fell in tendrils around her face as she slept. Occasionally, she would stir and mumble a word or two, but then she lay peacefully again in restful sleep.

Richard stayed the night, dozing off in the chair but awoke each time that Melanie would stir.

As the morning light streamed through the large windows, creating a pattern of stripes on the carpeting, Melanie suddenly awoke with a start. It was seven o'clock, and somewhere outside, a large hawk was protesting loudly. Melanie looked over to where Richard was slumped over in the chair, making low buzzing sounds as he slept. He appeared very peaceful in the midst of his slumber, but she knew that he hadn't slept well most of the night. Each time that she would awaken, there he'd be jumping to her side just in case she needed him.

What a wonderful and devoted friend he's become to me, she thought. At her time of great need, he remained with her, completely selfless and very generous with his attention. She was grateful for his good company and couldn't imagine what she would have done had she come home alone last night to find that Alan had committed suicide. How could she have faced this alone? And how would she tell the boys that their father was dead?

Just then, Richard opened his eyes and saw that Melanie was watching him. He got up from the chair and stretched his muscles, which had gotten stiff because he slept in a chair all night. He then walked over to the sofa and sat next to Melanie. "Are you feeling better this morning? You know, we've got a lot of things to do in the next few days."

"Yes, how well I know. This family has been through so many tragedies recently. But before we do anything else, I would like to go to the church down the road. Today is Sunday, and I really need the comfort that I always find there. Will you go with me, Richard?"

"Of course, Melanie, if you want, I will go with you."

"Thank you, Richard. Thank you for being so good to me. The boys will be home later this afternoon from camp, and it's going to be very difficult to tell them about their father. I'll have to give it some thought while we're at church. I still can't believe that this has happened." She fought back the tears that were welling up inside her, making her tremble as she spoke.

"Guess Alan thought it would be easier on you if he wasn't around," Richard said. "He couldn't face you after confessing the crimes he had committed. Besides, you know, Melanie, that he would have been disbarred. He'd have to go to prison, and what would he have done when he got out? He could never again lead the life to which he was accustomed, if he would even survive the prison term."

"It is going to be a long time before I can bring myself to forgive him, Richard. The boys will be very badly hurt by his thoughtless actions. I really dread having to tell them."

They drove to the church, which was approximately a couple of miles away from the Lambert house. Melanie went there often and would take the boys with her most of the time. Alan rarely went with them and would occasionally make plans with the boys on Sunday morning that would invariably prevent them from going with Melanie. He lacked the civilizing influence and strong moral code of ethics that come with practicing religion.

"Alan had always felt that religion was nothing but a superstition," Melanie said as they turned into the church parking lot. "He never found any need for it. I guess that was why he was able to do the things he did. His guilt feelings only surfaced when he had to face me. And to him, that must have been intolerable."

"You're probably right, Melanie. It must have been hell for him. I am sure that he felt you could never forgive him."

Chapter 26

It was almost four o'clock when the twin boys, chattering wildly about their weekend at Scout camp, walked in the front door. Each one tried to outdo the other by relating an exciting event that had occurred. There was much competition and sibling rivalry between the two boys. Being identical twins created a situation that was not unlike a continuous contest with the ultimate prize being recognition. Mark and Derek liked doing many of the same things but were dissimilar as much as they were similar. Mark was sensitive, discriminating, and emotional, whereas Derek was intemperate and somewhat uncompromising. Therefore, the resulting reaction of each boy to the news of their father's suicide was rather diverse.

"No, Mom, it can't be true. He's not dead!" Mark's voice began to rise to hysteria. Tears formed narrow rivulets down his cheeks. "You're wrong. He's alive. He's got to be! I love him too much, and I have so much to tell him."

Melanie put her arms around her son and held him close, trying to comfort him.

"How could he have committed suicide?" Derek protested aloud. "Didn't he care about us? Didn't he care how much he was hurting us?" Anger was written all over his boyish face.

Richard came over to Derek and held him by his shoulders. "Your father did what he felt was best. He didn't do it to hurt you. He spoke in a low monotone voice and tried to calm the boy. "He did some things that he wasn't proud of, and he felt that after you learned about them, you wouldn't feel the same way about him anymore. He felt that you wouldn't love him anymore, and he couldn't live with that. He probably would have been arrested and gone to prison. He ruined his life but didn't want to ruin yours too."

Melanie brought the two boys together. "Please understand and try to find it in your hearts to forgive him."

"I do forgive him, Mom," Mark responded. "But I miss him already. It doesn't matter what he did. I'll always remember him as a great guy."

"I'm pleased you feel that way, Mark," Melanie replied. "What about you, Derek?"

"Well, Mom, he had no right to take his life," Derek said. "He had no right to do that. What he did was worse than facing up to his crimes, and I wish he had been brave. What did he do that was so awful?"

Melanie carefully explained his part in the conspiracy and his reasons for committing the crimes. She didn't try to make excuses for him but merely stated the truth. She felt it was best to be honest with the boys rather than have them hear it from another source.

Melanie knew that Alan had been weak and dishonest and ungrateful for the opportunities he was given by her father. He had been unscrupulous in his dealings with Dr. Ulrich with a motive that was untenable. Melanie realized all of these things but would never divulge this to her sons. They were hurting badly enough. She would not destroy his memory for them completely.

"Dr. Ulrich was a former client of your father many years ago," Melanie related to the boys. "He lost the case for him and now felt that he owed him a favor. Your father went along with Dr. Ulrich's plan to stop the manufacture of a new drug which could have saved your grandfather's life, a drug that your uncle Ivan had developed. Dr. Ulrich had a drug of his own that he wanted to use that was also the first of its kind but not as good as Uncle Ivan's. It was a competition between the two men as to who would get the credit first for their drug. Your father didn't know that this would lead to your uncle Ivan's murder. He had nothing to do with that. What he did was write the threat notes that were given to your grandfather. Your grandfather was worried about the safety of our family, so he decided not to take either one of the drugs, and that is how he did not survive his illness."

"So Dad wrote the threat notes," Derek exclaimed.

"Yes, Derek, he did. He never intended to carry out any of the threats. He merely used them as a scare tactic. He also had someone from the hospital tap your grandfather's and uncle Ivan's phones. He also told me that he knew nothing of what happened to Uncle Ivan, and I believe him, and so should you. Dr. Ulrich and a man from the hospital named Joe Slater were arrested, and so your dad would have been arrested as well."

Melanie knew that the agony both of her sons were feeling was indescribable. But time would pass and heal the wounds. Their anguish for the loss of their father would dissipate with the routine of everyday life. In this devastating time of great need, Melanie was grateful that, to her, there existed a God, a compassionate one, to whom she could turn to for comfort, as she did earlier. Her father had paid a high price for his principles with a most precious commodity—his life. Similarly, her husband had paid the same price. But his was one of recrimination for the unprincipled life that he chose.

Once more, fate had placed her in the throes of bleak realization. She had lost another person who had been very dear and close to her heart. She could have felt bitterness for the cruel hand that she had been dealt and could have turned away from the merciless God who allowed this to happen. Instead, she knew that we each choose our own destiny with our God-given free will. We shape our lives in a manner that we each see fit. Occasionally, circumstances thrown in our path alter our sometimes complacent lives, bringing with them difficult hardships to endure. But by them, we are challenged and strengthened to face each new precipice.

Melanie would see to it that her sons would not look upon this dreadful incident grudgingly or with hatred but would use it as a stepping-stone toward building a stronger character, one that would have the capacity to choose a way of life that was more discriminating than the one their father had chosen.

Richard remained with them most of the day, being an enormous help to them all. Melanie was grateful for his company and his help in doing all the things she found too difficult.

Early this morning, he performed the difficult task of calling the family to let them know what had transpired since last evening's dinner party. Greg offered to help with all the arrangements, but Richard declined, saying that he would take care of everything along with Melanie. He assured Greg that everything was under control. Richard wanted to be the all-encompassing force that would bring Melanie and her sons through this unfortunate dilemma.

Recently, he had felt more than a mere friendship toward Melanie but was unable to express it. He hadn't completely realized his true feelings himself until last night, when he watched her sleep on the sofa, and again in the morning, when he saw her looking so very lovely with sleepy eyes and tussled hair. From that moment, Richard knew that he was in love with Melanie. Someday, he hoped that she would return his love and make him the focal point of her life. It would all take time, but he was a man who was gifted with patience.

Chapter 27

A few weeks later, after the funeral of Alan Lambert, Greg summoned Renée Bordeaux to his office to discuss a new plan he had that would drastically affect her future with the company. Renée sat on the large leather sofa in Greg's office, looking very demure and excited at the prospect of being assigned to a new project. That was all he had told her as he called her to his office. She was brimming with anticipation, wondering what it might be.

"What is this exciting new prospect that you have in store for me? I can hardly wait to hear about it, Greg."

He came over and sat down next to her on the sofa. Taking her hand in his, he said, "Our laboratory in France is finally complete, and as you know, I've been considering someone from this office to manage the sales department there. Well, I've made my choice at last and would like to announce the promotion at our board meeting this afternoon."

"Who are you referring to, Greg? You've been very mysterious about this entire thing."

"I didn't want anyone to know my decision until that particular person was contacted by me. Now I'd like to know, how would you like to be that person?"

"Me? But, Greg, I want to stay here, close to you. It is a wonderful opportunity for someone. At any other time, I would have welcomed this kind of promotion, but not now. Our relationship is just blossoming and will become something very beautiful, if given the chance."

"That's just it. Renée, I don't want to give our relationship a chance to blossom. I'm not a free man. You knew that from the outset. Renée, I still love my wife and wouldn't dream of hurting her. That is why this would be the best move for our relationship—to give it distance and to look at it more objectively. Please be realistic, Renée. It's never a good idea for two people working together in the same office to have such closeness. Somehow, word always gets around, and neither one of us can afford this kind of flagrant gossip. In fact, as far as I'm concerned, the best thing for our relationship would be separation. Besides, this promotion is something you really shouldn't turn down."

Renée appeared rather perturbed, weighing everything that Greg was saying. "You're probably correct in this, Greg, and I do respect your opinion, but for me, leaving you now would be very difficult."

"I really need you in France, Renée. The company needs your expertise there. Please be reasonable."

"Well, if you put it that way, I suppose I shouldn't refuse. Besides, I will get to see my family often. My parents are getting on, and they do miss me."

"That's more like it. Now I would like you to be ready to leave in the next week or two. So see if you can wrap things up around here, and we will make preparations for your transfer."

At the board meeting, Greg made the announcement that Renée would be the new executive of the sales department in Paris, France. Also, the new law firm that had been hired to replace the services of Trent, Randolph, and Lambert had been announced. Steve Warner, the chairman of the board, had given this all to the board for a vote. It was unanimous, and the vote was carried.

"Whatever happened to that Dr. Ulrich from the New England Cancer Institute who had been tied in with the conspiracy against this company?" asked Steve Warner.

"He was arrested and tried for Ivan's murder, along with a Joe Slater," Greg responded. "Dr. Ulrich hired Slater to do his dirty work for him in return for a position at the cancer institute. Slater wanted the position badly enough to succumb to the temptation. It was an unfortunate decision since it quickly brought Dr. Ulrich's brilliant career to an end. As for Dr. Paul Glasser, he was questioned and released since he wasn't aware of how deeply the conspiracy had gone. All he was asked to do was to get something from Marissa of importance to her, and he did. It was finally returned to her, and she was never in any great danger, although he was fined for his part in it and for taking advantage of Marissa. He will also have to do some community service, which is a good thing."

"As for the formula, we were able to retrieve some of Ivan's notes. They will prove to be a help in replacing the miracle formula on which he so diligently worked."

"I'm glad the investigation is finally over and settled," replied Steve. "It must have been very painful for you and your family to be put through all of this tragedy. But, Greg, it is time to forgive and forget. It is time to journey into the future."

"You are absolutely right, Steve. We will all do just that."

* * *

At the airport, Greg and Renée were working their way through the crowd of people bustling in all directions, getting baggage checked and rushing to make their flights.

"This past week simply flew by, Greg, my love." Renée looked up at this tall, blondish man she adored and realized that she was leaving and wouldn't be seeing him for quite some time. "When will you be making an inspection of our Paris laboratory? We will be looking forward to your visit, and I might add your approval," Renée said whimsically. "I'm feeling a bit shaky, Greg. Will you hold me? You know how reluctant I am to leave you."

Greg took her in his arms and held her tenderly. "I'll miss you too, Renée. You're the kind of woman of whom most men can only dream. I've been lucky enough to have experienced your closeness with so much grand passion. Before I met you, I thought I'd never experience that again. It's been wonderful, Renée."

She moved closer to him and sought his mouth with hers. Greg felt her body quiver in response to her closeness, and she longed for him desperately. But this was why he was sending her away. For as long as she was around, he would always want her as well. He had to finally let go. He owed his wife, Vanessa, some allegiance, even though he might never again be able to work up the passion that he now felt so strongly for Renée.

"Love me, Greg. Keep me always in your heart. I'll always be thinking of you. Visit me often, sweetheart, and I will welcome you with warm and open arms. And one day, Greg, I will have you for keeps. Thank you for the memories I take with me."

Greg watched her as she broke away and walked toward the line of people who were getting ready to be checked by security. He saw her delicate small figure then disappear from view.

In a little while, the plane lifted its huge silver fuselage toward the vast blue sky and gradually became smaller and smaller, leaving a vapor trail until it disappeared beyond the amorphous clouds.

Epilogue

Greg sat in his office at Stone Pharmaceutical Labs, thinking back to what had evolved within his company as well as his family. Taken to paraphrasing from his favorite author, Charles Dickens, *A Tale of Two Cities*, his mind began to wander. These were the best of times, and these were the worst of times—this line certainly described his personal as well as his business history.

The best of times, of course, related to the success of his company even during these difficult economic times. He had expanded to Paris, France, which proved to be a success story in itself. That was two years ago, and now he was looking to expand further on foreign soil. He already had the United States as well as Canada.

The worst of times was the loss of his father, MacGregor Stone, who founded the company and made it a success, the success on which Greg had continued to build. A handful of men conspired to compete and threatened the lives of his family. The conspiracy that resulted in the murder of his uncle Ivan in a fiery car crash had caused much pain for the family as well as the company. He was the scientist who developed an anti-cancer drug, the information of which, had been destroyed in the fire. However, it was all able to be recovered through notes he had left behind. They were not complete, but through the ingenious efforts of his scientific staff, the drug was able to be recreated. The other loss was his brother-in-law, who felt pressured to become a part of the conspiracy, not knowing the extent of the evil that had developed. He could not find it possible to continue his life as it was with his family due to his guilt, therefore ending it in a suicide.

Greg's daughter, Marissa, had also been subject to danger with the tentacles of the conspiracy reaching out for her. Luckily, she was spared, and no real harm had come to her. Her experience had matured her and helped her to make better choices.

Marissa, had graduated from Boston College and was now working at Stone Pharmaceutical Labs, learning the business and proving to be a good asset to the company with fresh ideas. Greg was more than elated with her progress ever since he hired her as a part of his staff.

As for his brief affair with Renée Bordeaux, one of his executives in the Paris office, he had never revealed this to his wife, Vanessa. He regretted the affair and felt that it was a mistake. Due to the fact that she was his employee and for that short time in Paris, he felt that he lost his allegiance to his wife. He could not fathom telling Vanessa and hurting her so dreadfully since the affair was no longer significant to him.

Two years made a big difference in his life. The vicissitudes of the past changed him to appreciate his family more so than ever before. All of the adversity had finally deprived misfortune of its power. His work was important and always would be; however, his family took precedence over everything. They always would.

His mother, who was placed on the board of directors, was an inspiration to him too. She was almost able to read his very thoughts. He found her to be extremely intuitive as to what he wanted from the board and was able to move them to vote in the right direction. He found her to be absolutely uncanny. His father was accurate in suggesting that she be placed on the board.

His sister, Melanie, who lost her husband, Alan, two years ago due to suicide, had fallen in love with Dr. Richard Brooks, Greg's longtime friend. They were very compatible with each other, and her twins grew to love him just as much.

What wonders did exist for his company. He was filled with exciting admiration and amazement for a company that, by its virtue of being outstanding, had truly succeeded and progressed.

About the Author

Sylvia Stachura's career has included working at local hospitals as an administrative medical secretary, data coordinator, and spent time working with medical records.

She worked at the nationally renowned Roswell Park Cancer Institute in Buffalo, New York (RPCI). It provided a rude awakening as to the profound suffering the patients were experiencing, the magnitude of which she had never witnessed before.

While at RPCI, she was given extensive instruction in the cancer disease process, as well as the treatments that were available at the time. She continued to work there after being married and until their children were born. For a short time, she worked at Sisters of Charity Hospital, editing and transcribing surgical reports.

She later returned to RPCI as a data coordinator for a nutritional study on laryngectomy patients, who had cancer of the larynx and had their voice box removed. She also worked at the

Buffalo General Hospital as an Administrative Secretary for three Cardiologists in the Cardiac Angiology Department.

Her schooling included attending Erie Community College focusing on medical technology courses. She developed an interest in writing after attending local writing workshops and conferences.

Sylvia lives in Williamsville, New York with her husband, Ed, who is a retired civil engineer. They have two grown children, six grandchildren, and two great grandsons.

Milton Keynes UK
Ingram Content Group UK Ltd.
UKHW011855041124
450744UK00010B/252